P9-DSY-602

Other Books by the Same Author

ACCENT ON APRIL

ALMOST LIKE SISTERS

ANGEL ON SKIS

THE BOY NEXT DOOR

A BREATH OF FRESH AIR

THE COUNTRY COUSIN

FANCY FREE

JENNY KIMURA

MYSTERY AT LOVE'S CREEK

PASSPORT TO ROMANCE

THE SCARLET SAIL

STARS IN HER EYES

A TIME FOR TENDERNESS

Published by William Morrow and Company

THE BLACK SPANIEL MYSTERY

A GIRL CAN DREAM

GOING ON SIXTEEN

LASSO YOUR HEART

LOVE, LAURIE

PAINTBOX SUMMER

PUPPY STAKES

6 ON EASY STREET

SPRING COMES RIDING

SPURS FOR SUZANNA

A TOUCH OF MAGIC

TWO'S COMPANY

Published by The Westminster Press

Mystery in Marrakech

by BETTY CAVANNA

William Morrow and Company

Published simultaneously in Canada by
George J. McLeod Limited, Toronto.

Printed in the United States of America.

Library of Congress Catalog Card Number 68-25482

Mystery in Marrakech

BETTY CAVANNA grew up in Haddonfield, New Jersey, and was graduated from Douglass College, where she majored in journalism. It was during her work for Westminster Press in Philadelphia that she became interested in writing stories herself, and in 1943 she became a full-time writer of books for young people. She holds an honorary membership in Phi Beta Kappa for her outstanding contribution to the field of juvenile literature. In private life Miss Cavanna is Mrs. George Russell Harrison. She and her husband live in Concord, Massachusetts.

One

Marrakech!

The name was so romantic, so infinitely mysterious, that Deborah's hands grew clammy with excitement as her imagination conjured up dreams of snake charmers and veiled women, Oriental bazaars and bearded Arabs, camel caravans and international espionage. "I can't believe it," she whispered again to her roommate, who was placidly unwrapping one of the mints passed around by the airline stewardess. "I still can't believe I'm here!"

"You aren't—yet." Felicia, a timid flyer, wriggled in the seat beside Deborah, stretched her long legs, and tried to peer past her traveling companion's shoulder to catch a glimpse of the High Atlas Mountains, still snow-capped even though it was mid-June in Morocco, and likely to be ninety degrees Fahrenheit on the plain.

"But we will be, in just a few minutes. See! The flaps are down."

To see anything past the obtrusive shoulder was impossible. However, conditioned by a year of living with Dizzy Driscoll at Abbott Academy, Felicia didn't complain. She expected and even enjoyed her roommate's enthusiasm, so long as she didn't have to participate.

"Look!" Belatedly sitting back and allowing Felicia a tilted view of the plane's wing, an olive orchard, and a high red wall, Dizzy asked, "How can you just sit there munching on mints? Why aren't you jumping up and down like me?"

"For one thing, my seat belt is fastened, and for another I'm taller than you, Dizzy, and my knees have gone to sleep." Felicia yawned to assuage the tightness in her eardrums and added, "I've been here before, remember? But I'm just as excited, in my own way. I'll be awfully glad to see Mother and Father—and Rick."

The reference to Felicia's older brother, whom Dizzy knew only through a fading snapshot tucked into the corner of the mirror they had shared for two semesters, made her suddenly concerned for her appearance. She opened her purse, applied fresh lipstick, looked with her usual dismay at her shining, freckled nose, and searched vainly for a comb with which to tame her fluffy blond hair.

"You needn't put on an act for Rick," said Felicia mildly. "He's apt to appear in shorts and a T-shirt."

Flushing, Dizzy snapped her compact shut. Sometimes a roommate was too much like an alter ego. "I'm only trying to look presentable for your parents," she retorted, and could tell from Felicia's expression that the excuse was lame.

The runway reached up to meet the plane, and the pilot settled down jerkily, applied his brakes, then taxied to the terminal, which to Dizzy looked little larger than a New England barn, very small and insignificant for a city of nearly 300,000. Heat waves pulsated visibly above the tarmac, and the mountains had disappeared in the haze, making her wonder fleetingly if the jagged peaks had been a mirage.

Felicia finally managed to bestir herself and gather up her raincoat, her camera, and the thin paper bag bursting with more than a dozen paperbacks acquired at Orly. "In Marrakech during the heat of the day," she had predicted with almost Victorian quaintness, "there will be nothing to do but read."

When they had been scampering from one end of the Paris airport to the other, in an effort to see everything that could be seen in the hour they were on the ground, Deborah had cheerfully ignored this warning. But now, as the flimsy bag finally tore and the books scattered in all directions, she was enlisted to help gather them up and cart them, a bulky armful added to her own hand luggage, from the plane.

The throng at the gate was not large, but it was

remarkable in its diversity. There were indeed veiled women and men in long jellabas and white turbans, but there were also fashionable Frenchwomen and swarthy businessmen in dark, summer-weight Western suits. There were ragged, big-eyed Arab children and smartly uniformed policemen; and finally there was Rick, in sneakers and shorts as Felicia had predicted, edging toward them to rescue the books Dizzy was about to drop.

"Hi! You must be Dizzy," he said the moment he had greeted his sister. His merry brown eyes regarded her appraisingly. "Felicia didn't tell me you were such a *little* girl."

"Five-foot five isn't little," Dizzy demurred. "I only look little because—"

"Because I'm so large," Felicia finished equably. She was indeed taller than her brother, statuesque and fair, looking older than her sixteen years, just as Dizzy looked younger. They were alike only in the fact both were blond.

Rick laughed, then pecked his sister affectionately on the cheek. "You're not getting any smaller," he agreed without quibble. "I kind of resent being the runt of the family, so I'll enjoy having you to look down on, Dizzy. Whew, it's hot. Let's get going, shall we? Give me your checks and I'll pick up the bags."

Surreptitiously, Dizzy watched Felicia's brother as he walked away, weaving through the throng with a springy step that indicated either excessive energy or cockiness. Secretly, she was disappointed in Rick, who was a sophomore at Dartmouth and presumably sophisticated. She had visualized him as taller, with fair, smooth hair like his sister's, and a sort of rugged good looks. Instead, as she could see even from a distance, his sandy hair flew up in uncontrollable cowlicks, his nose was short and impudent, his smile winning but tentative, as though begging for encouragement. Actually, he *is* rather like a puppy, Dizzy decided. He made her feel protective rather than romantic. Unconsciously, she sighed, then recovered her poise as she caught Felicia watching her. "Isn't it nice to be taken care of?" she asked with a smile.

Since the girls had gone through customs in Casablanca, where they had changed from a jet to a Royal Air Maroc plane, there was no delay. Within a few minutes Dizzy and Felicia were being whisked along a broad straight road toward the city, which rose so gently from the Haouz Plain that it seemed like a shimmering extension of the red earth.

Rick acted both as chauffeur and guide, secure in his experience with Morocco, where his family had been living for almost a year. Ignoring the fact that his sister was equally qualified, he pointed out to Dizzy the city ramparts behind the olive and palm groves, and named a minaret rising against the blue sky in the distance. "That's the Koutoubia, and it's one landmark you're bound to remember. It's like the Eiffel Tower in Paris or our Statue of Liberty. The Moroccans think it's the greatest."

Dizzy leaned forward to peer out of the car at the square tower. "It is pretty impressive," she agreed, but it was the passing scene rather than the city's architecture that fascinated her. There were donkeys laden with staggering piles of baskets and pottery water jars, Arabs curled up asleep under the scanty shade of an occasional eucalyptus tree, urchins equipped with staffs to beat their flocks of skinny sheep back off the highway, and then—lo and behold!—the first camel she had ever seen outside a zoo.

She positively gurgled with delight as they passed the tall beast, who was walking superciliously ahead of his master, curling his lip at an occasional car, then peering down at the stony, hard-packed earth in a vain attempt to discover a clump of edible grass. "I want to ride one!" Dizzy cried. "Oh, Felicia, will you take my picture on a camel so I can send it to my family? Me on a camel—imagine! Won't it be fun?"

Felicia shuddered. "Fun? They have fleas, all of them."

Her brother chuckled. "So what? You can take a bath."

"I wouldn't miss riding on a camel." Dizzy felt indignant. "What did you come to Morocco for?"

"Mother and Father insisted, remember?" Felicia replied evenly. She was mopping her damp forehead with a handkerchief. "I loathe hot countries. You don't think I'd come here by choice?"

Dizzy always kept forgetting that her roommate was so widely traveled, even though they were the same age. For the past eight years Felicia had spent every summer abroad, as her father's consulting jobs led him from Saudi Arabia to Egypt, from Japan to Brazil, and finally to Morocco. Here Dr. Harding was spending his sabbatical, on leave for a full year from the Massachusetts Institute of Technology, where he was a petroleum geologist in the Department of Earth Sciences. Just what this meant Dizzy didn't quite understand, but she gathered that Felicia's father was in great demand as a scientific advisor to oil interests in underdeveloped countries, and that his assignment in Marrakech had something to do with the Moroccan government, headed by King Hassan II.

Lucky for me, she thought, that the Hardings decided Felicia would be happier spending a second summer in Marrakech if she brought a friend along. The temperature could climb to 100 in the shade, and she wouldn't complain. Abbott Academy seemed as remote as the moon from this romantic, red-walled city. She felt as though a magic carpet had whisked her back in time to biblical days, when ancestors of these same people must have worn similar robes and turbans and sat back on the rumps of their donkeys in the selfsame way.

Rick was still bubbling with information. "This is

the Mamounia," he said as they passed an entrance drive swooping up to a big hotel. "Winston Churchill's bailiwick. He used to come here each winter to paint. There's a slick swimming pool in the back, but you can't see it from here."

What Dizzy could see was a line of waiting carriages, and she clapped her hands spontaneously. "Oh, I want to ride in one of those too!"

"You will," Rick promised. "If you need transportation you have two choices—a *petit taxi* or a *calèche*."

Calèche. Dizzy filed the French term in her mind for future reference as Felicia said, "The Mamounia's also the scene of one of the best Hitchcock mysteries. We have the book around the house somewhere, but I can't seem to recall the title. What is it, Rick?"

Felicia's brother shook his head. "You know suspense fiction isn't my department. How you can read all that—that fluff," he said, reconsidering a word he obviously had intended to use, "is more than I can see."

His sister shrugged. "It passes the time."

"Wastes it, you mean."

Felicia raised her eyebrows. "What do you call playing tennis?"

"I call it exercise, and it would do you good."

Dizzy smiled to herself. Felicia disliked exercise almost as much as she loathed hot weather. At school she used up all her free cuts on gym, and regarded

Dizzy with misgiving whenever she went off with her racquet.

"Patrick dear, stop trying to reform me," Felicia said now. "Dizzy will doubtless play tennis with you." To herself she murmured, " 'Mad dogs and Englishmen go out in the midday sun.' "

Rick's merry dark eyes sought Dizzy's. "It happens that we don't have a court," he said, "so you're safe."

"Only for the moment," Felicia said in warning. "Rick is full of misdirected verve."

"I consider that slander!" Rick objected, slapping the wheel. "Pay no attention to her, Dizzy. She's just jealous because I'm three years older than she is and can still manage to move at more than a slow crawl."

Dizzy laughed. Having expected to be quite in awe of Felicia's brother, she was still surprised at finding him so disarmingly simple. Why, he seemed closer to her own age than to the superior eminence of twenty, which he would reach before the end of the summer. If she had been daydreaming about a possible romantic encounter under the swaying palms of Marrakech she might as well forget it. At least with Patrick Harding, Jr. He was nice enough, but scarcely her beau ideal.

Turning off the broad avenue along which they had been traveling, Rick skirted an enormous square called by a strange name that Felicia had to spell for her roommate—and which Dizzy promptly forgot—Djemaa-el-Fna.

"It's quiet now," Rick said, "but you should see this place around six P.M. Wow, it's really swinging!"

Dizzy looked puzzled. "What do you mean?"

"It's like a perpetual fun fair," Felicia explained. "For ages and ages public entertainers have come here—snake charmers and sword swallowers and fire eaters, acrobats from Taroudant, white-robed Berber dancers, storytellers. I could go on and on."

"Do," suggested Dizzy.

Felicia's eyes grew less abstracted than usual. "You have to see it to believe it, but at dusk this square is so alive with people that from a distance they look like ants, all gathered in fluid circles around the entertainers. You get a marvelous view from up there," she said, pointing to the balcony of a café. "The smells are completely Eastern and the rumble of voices is like background music. Then there are drums beating and cymbals clanging and the tinkle of water sellers' bells. . . ."

"Sis, you should be a writer," Rick said, only half teasing.

"That's what I keep telling her," Dizzy seconded. "I get A on all the themes she revises for me." Then her attention was caught by a closer glimpse of the Koutoubia as Rick turned the car toward another part of town.

Past walls draped with bougainvillea and houses muffled in groves of olive and orange trees they sped.

Date palms soared high into the blue sky, donkeys and their drivers dozed on their feet as they ambled along, and the more fortunate people of Marrakech stirred lazily, aware that the siesta hours were drawing to a close.

"Here we are," Rick announced importantly a few minutes later, pulling up before a wrought-iron portal in a high rose-colored wall. A pantalooned gardener laid down his rake and came over to unlock and open the gate, grinning toothlessly. "*Merci beaucoup*," Rick called as he eased the car through and pulled up before a broad entrance walk flanked by huge water-lily pools and leading to the door of a house that looked to Dizzy like a small palace.

She gasped in spontaneous delight and cried, "Isn't it perfectly heavenly!" The overall impression was of pale pink plaster walls and wrought-iron balconies festooned with climbing tropical vines bearing an abundance of blue flowers. Palms soared above the tiled roofs, and a peacock stepped arrogantly along the border of one of the pools toward a bridge crossing a larger pond in the distance.

Rick tooted the horn and reached for the girls' luggage as the tall double entrance doors were flung open and Mrs. Harding hurried out, her arms forthstretched in greeting. She was a slender woman, not quite as tall as Felicia, with fine gray eyes and suntanned skin, set off by a pale green cotton dress and matching sandals, which looked so thoroughly Bostonian that Dizzy was amused. Here was a door through which a wife of Harun al-Raschid could have walked but instead an American mother appeared.

"Felicia darling!" Mrs. Harding gathered her daughter briefly into her arms. "Deborah! How nice of you to come." Her voice was crisp yet truly welcoming and her manner, like Felicia's, was slightly formal.

While Dizzy was expressing her delight at being invited, Rick, with a display of strength, managed to pick up all four of the girls' bulky suitcases. "Where'll I take the luggage, Mum?" he asked, clowning, when there was a break in the conversation.

Mrs. Harding shook her head and smiled in pretended despair. "Patrick, put those down. You know Ali will get them." She led the girls into a marble-floored entrance hall and spoke in French to an approaching servant, who was wearing a starched white jacket above voluminous black bloomers and yellow Moroccan leather slippers. "I've put you across the hall from Felicia, dear," she then said to Dizzy. "After enduring her midnight reading habits for a full school year I think you deserve a rest."

Still feeling as though she were walking through a dream, Dizzy followed Ali to a second-floor bedroom at the back of the house. The room had a decorative wood ceiling and its own private balcony overlooking a flower garden and olive orchard to a view of the High Atlas, remote and shimmering forty miles away.

"I'm sure you'll want to bathe and rest," said Mrs. Harding as she came along the hall with Felicia. "It just happens that we're having a small dinner party tonight—a business affair really—but our guests won't be arriving until eight, so you'll have three hours." She spoke directly to Dizzy. "I hope you won't be too tired to join us?"

Tired? Dizzy had never felt more wide-awake in her life, but in view of the fact that Felicia was trying to stifle a series of compulsive yawns she went into her room and obediently closed the door.

Slowly she unpacked, soaked for half an hour in a tub of cold water, then, refreshed, slipped into a negligee and walked softly out to her balcony.

The tiled floor felt cool on her bare feet because by now the sun had slipped down the western sky, leaving half the compound in shadow. The old gardener still worked with his rake, smoothing out footprints in the gravel paths and accumulating a small harvest of dead leaves. Overhead a flight of white birds that looked like egrets passed swiftly, their breasts painted with the oranges and pinks of the dying sun. They made no sound, but they seemed to know precisely where they were going, and they were in a hurry.

Dizzy leaned on the railing and tried to fix the scene indelibly in her memory. It was so quiet, so peaceful, so remarkably beautiful. . . .

Unexpectedly, from a thicket of hibiscus near the

garden wall, came a sibilant "Hsst!" and Dizzy started. The Arab gardener straightened his bent back and glanced toward the house, then carried his rake slowly toward the direction of the voice, just as an eerie wail erupted in the distance, a high-pitched chant taken up here and there all over the city. Dizzy listened, fascinated, because Felicia had told her that this was the most memorable sound in Marrakech. Five times each day she would hear it. From the minarets of many mosques the muezzins were calling the faithful to prayer.

Dizzy half expected the gardener to kneel, facing Mecca, but he hurried on into the shadows. Suddenly Dizzy shivered, filled with an unreasoning apprehension at the strangeness of everything. This was North Africa, a land of Berbers and Arabs, of black Bedouin tents, vast deserts and unexplored mountains, of witch doctors, widespread poverty and great opulence. What was she doing here? Why had she come?

Two

Dizzy's misgivings were short-lived. By the time she had finished dressing she felt cheerful and full of anticipation at the prospect of an adult dinner party in this enchanting house.

Ready to go downstairs promptly at eight o'clock, she knocked on the door across the hall and was rewarded with Felicia's languid, "Come in."

Her roommate, in a short white slip, was lying flat on the bed reading a paperback. "Hey!" Dizzy scolded. "Do you know what time it is?"

Felicia put down the book reluctantly and swung her feet to the floor. "There's no real hurry," she advised Dizzy. "Morocco's like Brazil. Everybody gets everywhere at least half an hour late. Everybody except my father, that is."

"Well, come on. I'll wait for you."

Although she moved deliberately, it took Felicia only a few minutes to slip into a sleeveless white dress and brush her long, shining hair so that it fell straight to her rounded shoulders.

Dizzy disapproved of her roommate's plumpness, but she always envied her hair. It was so luxuriant and manageable, easy to arrange, while her own was too curly by far. She was forced to wear it short and its fluffiness, combined with her blue eyes, gave her the appearance of a surprised kitten.

Nevertheless she tried to look as grown-up as possible when she descended the stairs and was introduced to Dr. Harding, who was pacing impatiently back and forth across the broad entrance hall. She could tell at once that he was a vigorous man, in spite of his reputation as a scholar. His frame, like Rick's, was square-shouldered and stocky, his eyes keen, and his manner brisk and businesslike. "Glad you're here to keep my daughter out of mischief," he said to Dizzy as he shook hands.

Since mischief was the last thing that ever attracted Felicia, Dizzy accepted this as the pleasantry it was intended to be. She smiled up at him and promised, "I'll do my best," with which Dr. Harding patted her on the shoulder while Felicia took her hand and drew her in the direction of the dining room. Through an arched doorway Dizzy could see Mrs. Harding moving around a long table sparkling with crystal and set for ten. She was sorting through a number of place cards distractedly.

"It just isn't possible, Mrs. Harding," came a voice from an invisible advisor. "If you want the doctor at one end of the table and you mean to be at the other you've got to bunch up the Russian and that Ayrab like I told you earlier."

Momentarily taken aback by the West Virginia accent, Dizzy realized this must be Louella, the Negro cook who always accompanied the Hardings abroad. "My father hates continental breakfasts," Felicia had explained on the trip over. "He takes Louella along to cook his bacon and eggs."

It must be nice to have a family retainer, Dizzy thought when she was led to meet an ample, smiling woman who first gathered Felicia against her bosom in a bear hug, then took one of Dizzy's hands in both her own. "Such a mite of a thing," Louella crooned after the proper introduction. "We got to fatten you up a bit, now you're here."

Meanwhile Mrs. Harding apparently had come to some decisions concerning the dinner-party seating arrangement, because miraculously the cards were placed on the table a moment before her husband called from the hall. Louella disappeared into the kitchen, and Rick came bounding down the stairs just as the first guest arrived.

Ali, who was now wearing a red fez, raced his employer to the door. Dr. Harding won, which seemed to amuse his wife rather than annoy her. "Formalities are lost on my dear husband," she confessed in a whisper to Dizzy, who noticed that she looked affectionate instead of embarrassed.

On the threshold stood a tall angular woman with dark auburn hair, who looked very French and was fashionably dressed. "Odette!" Dr. Harding cried. "I'm glad you're early. I want to talk to you for a few minutes before the others come." There followed a mild flurry of greetings to the young people, an introduction to Dizzy, and a hasty cheek-touching by the two women, who apparently knew one another well. Then Dr. Harding led the newcomer off to a small room at the back of the hall that was apparently the library.

Dizzy watched the Frenchwoman walk away, admiring her carriage. She was enormously impressed because she had been presented to the Countess de Redier, the first titled person that she had ever met.

"Does the Countess live here in Marrakech?" she asked Rick in a whisper.

"Yes. Over near the Djemaa-el-Fna. She works for Pop as a sort of confidential secretary. It's great to have somebody who speaks perfect French and English and a little Arabic."

"She is a very dear friend of ours as well as being my husband's secretary," put in Mrs. Harding, then glanced at Rick reprovingly. "Patrick, I have asked you not to refer to your father as Pop."

"Sorry, Mum." Rick grinned impishly and winked at Dizzy. It was obvious that he could not be cut to Felicia's mold of conformity. In his son Dr. Harding's vigor had been transmuted into breeziness.

As Mrs. Harding turned away to greet another arrival, Dizzy felt puzzled. Why was a countess working as a secretary? She had always thought of nobility as rich. But before she could consult either Felicia or Rick on this point she found herself being introduced to a burly, pink-cheeked gentleman named Mr. Leontov, who spoke with a thick Russian accent and kept touching his bald head as though he were brushing away a fly. His manner was courteous but distant, and he seemed to find the presence of the young people disconcerting. "It's a pleasure," came through his moustache rather thinly as he bent over Felicia's and Deborah's hands.

Two Arabs, in immaculate white turbans and jellabas worn over Western shirts and neckties, came up the walk together. One was a tall man, Dr. Mohammed el Hazziz, who wore his importance with dignity, and Dizzy was not surprised that he turned out to be a member of the King's cabinet. He certainly looked the part of a high government official. Accompanying him was Bou Hamida, a slender, hawk-nosed young man with a flashing smile. Apparently he was connected with Dr. Harding's office, since everyone in the family seemed to know him quite well.

James Carlsmith, a hearty Texan, arrived last, hurrying into the living room, to which everyone had adjourned for aperitifs, with an apologetic grin. "I'm terribly sorry, Grace," he said in explanation to his hostess, "but I had to wait for a phone call coming through from the States." In contrast to the Russian, Mr. Carlsmith seemed delighted to have the young people present, and when Dizzy found herself on his left at dinner, with Rick on her other side, she felt relieved.

In any event, it appeared that very little was expected of her. The men, rather than the women, controlled the conversation, and although Dr. Harding made several abortive attempts to keep the talk general, it repeatedly shifted to the subject that interested them all—oil.

"I understand," said Mr. Carlsmith, speaking across the table to Mr. Leontov, "that today's newspaper reports there is a corps of more than two hundred Soviet petroleum experts and technicians in Algeria. I suppose they're helping the Algerian government develop the oil deposits recently found there?"

The Russian looked deprecating. "Perhaps, like many news reports, this is a trifle exaggerated," he suggested.

"In any event it sounds as though you people have your hands full," said Mr. Carlsmith, laughing, and then turned to his hostess with a compliment concerning her beautiful flowers.

Mr. Leontov did not look amused. He said to Dr.

Harding, "It would be foolish to pretend that oil is less important for the Soviets than it is for the Americans."

"Extremely foolish," agreed his host, "which leads me to suggest that the report should not be discounted. I just hope that another border quarrel will not develop. The one in 1963 was most unpleasant for everyone concerned."

Louella's dinner was delicious, and Dizzy was hungry, so she found herself listening with only one ear, but it was apparent that beneath a superficial politeness a good deal of sparring was going on between the Russian and the two Americans. Dr. Hazziz said very little, and Bou Hamida quite rudely ignored Mr. Leontov, who was on his right, in favor of a dialogue conducted in an undertone with Felicia, who appeared to intrigue him. Rick listened to the men, as did the Countess and Mrs. Harding, until over dessert the conversation began to sound like a rather angry debate in the United Nations.

Then, a practiced hostess, Mrs. Harding rescued the situation by pushing back her chair and suggesting that mint tea would be served on the terrace.

Mint tea, not coffee? Dizzy was surprised, and quite unprepared for the typically Moroccan ceremony that followed. As soon as everyone was seated, Ali appeared with a huge silver tray set with an ornate teapot and ten slender gilded glasses, into which he poured, with great precision, long streams of a hot amber liquid with a tantalizing aroma. With all the unction of a Chevalier de Tastevin he passed the tray first to his host and then to the other men before offering it to the ladies. Dizzy found her glass warm to the touch and she sniffed the mint aroma before tasting the brew, then gave a happy sigh. "Mm!"

The tea proved delightfully cooling and thirst-quenching, and she accepted another glass gratefully, then turned to look out over the pond where lanterns were being carried to the arched bridge. A trio of white-robed musicians followed, and from an assortment of exotic instruments, one of which looked like a reed flute and another like a two-stringed mandolin, there issued a high-pitched series of chords with a strangely primitive sound.

Rick moved over to lean close to Dizzy. "They're playing Berber music," he told her, and indicated the third player. "See his drum? It's called a *bendir*, and it's made by stretching a goatskin over a jar. He's hitting it first with his fingers and then with his palm. Sort of gets you, doesn't it?"

Dizzy nodded. The beat was indeed insistent, seeming to strike her in the stomach. Different from anything she had ever heard, she couldn't evaluate it, but she knew the music was disquieting. Surreptitiously she glanced around at the faces lit by the terrace torches and once more she felt very far from her home town in suburban Connecticut. Somehow the Russian looked sinister, the Arabs swarthy and mysterious, and even

Mr. Carlsmith and Dr. Harding seemed remote and preoccupied. She wasn't sorry when the men excused themselves and retired to the library.

Only Rick remained with the women, and as soon as it was courteous to do so his mother sent him over to thank the musicians and suggest that they might disperse. Dizzy drew her chair closer to her hostess and the Countess. The stars seemed yellow and low hanging and the night a black velvet tent that might collapse and smother her.

Conscious of her roommate's reaction, Felicia smiled. "What's the matter, cat walk over your grave?"

Dizzy shook her head. "But I feel like a character escaped from the Arabian Nights."

Overhearing, the Countess smiled. "Marrakech is more beautiful than Bagdad ever was, and the Moroccans are marvelous people, kind and courteous and very honest. You'll grow to love them," she promised. "You wait and see."

She rose and turned to her hostess. "I'm afraid I must say *au revoir*. Your husband asked me to be on hand early in the morning. There are several last-minute arrangements to make."

Last minute for what? Dizzy wondered, but of course it would be impolite to ask. Only after the Countess and the other guests had left, was she given an inkling of what the dinner party had been all about.

Then, accompanying Felicia and Rick to the library to say good night to Dr. Harding, she was invited to sit down. "I think you children may be interested to know that our oil negotiations are reaching a climax," he said, with an air of great satisfaction. "As you may have gathered, Mr. Leontov has been hoping to persuade the Moroccan cabinet to engage Russian help in the search for oil. Nearly a year ago I came to Morocco on a similar mission for Amarab Petroleum, of which Mr. Carlsmith is a vice-president. Our work has been delayed because, although King Hassan and most of his cabinet tend to lean toward the West, a strong group favors the Arab bloc and Soviet cooperation.

"This evening Dr. Hazziz broke the news to Mr. Leontov that the cabinet has decided to cooperate with us. Mr. Carlsmith is returning to America, and as soon as possible I shall take my assistant, Bou Hamida, and our prospecting group down to the Sahara to start looking for oil."

Although she tried to listen carefully, Dizzy was so sleepy that she could scarcely keep her head erect, and Felicia was definitely nodding. After all it had been a long and exciting day. Fortunately, Mrs. Harding was completely aware of the girls' exhaustion, and at the first break in her husband's monologue she managed to have them excused. "Sleep as late as you like, Deborah," she suggested. "When you're ready for breakfast ring the bell by your bed. It will be brought to you on a tray."

"Thank you. That sounds heavenly," Dizzy replied. She felt like a pampered princess as she walked upstairs. Breakfast in bed! Only when she was recovering from an illness had she ever been served breakfast in bed, and then she had not been very hungry. Now the prospect delighted her more than she could say.

The girls parted before their respective doors, while Rick tramped off to his own bedroom in the opposite wing of the house. Over the garden a half moon swung, illuminating the pale gravel paths as it rode above the swaying palms. A dog barked, a rooster mistook the light of the moon for dawn and crowed loudly, a donkey brayed unhappily in the distance, but Dizzy didn't attempt to separate or identify the various sounds. She stepped out of her dress, flinging it to the nearest chair, dropped her underwear to the floor, and pulled on the pajamas spread out like a butterfly on her turned-down bed. Even luxury no longer interested her. Throwing herself on top of the coverlet she fell sound asleep.

Just when she awakened she didn't know, but she stirred, then wriggled uncomfortably because she was cold. The air had changed, and a chill night breeze was sweeping down from the mountains. The light of the moon no longer touched her balcony, and the room was dark as pitch. Shivering, she slipped under the covers and pulled them up around her neck, then lay curled in a ball, tense and trying to will herself back to sleep.

She missed Felicia, to whose light snoring in the next bed she had grown accustomed during these past eight months. She also missed the familiar night sounds of Abbott Academy—the creak of floorboards as a restless student walked down the hall to the bathroom, the hum of a high-flying jet winging over New England, the rustle of oak leaves caressing the windowpane.

Yet she was glad school was over and she was thrilled at being here in Morocco, embarked on the first real adventure of her life. To go abroad on guided tours as some of her classmates were doing no longer seemed enviable. How much more exciting it was to be living like a resident of Marrakech rather than like a tourist. What a privilege to be invited and how lucky she was her parents had allowed her to come. Now thoroughly awake, Dizzy opened her eyes in the hope that it would soon be dawn and another exciting day would begin.

But the darkness was still thick and she thought idly that a cloud must have drifted over the moon. I must send Mother and Dad a postcard first thing in the morning, Dizzy reminded herself, and could picture them reading it together, seated side by side on the yellow damask sofa, one dark head graying at the temples and the other no longer quite so blond as it once had been. She'd find a card with a camel on it for Nancy, too, and post it to her younger sister at camp, the same Maine riding camp to which she herself had gone—Deborah Driscoll and now Nancy Driscoll in Cabin Nine.

Shifting position, Dizzy closed her eyes determinedly once more. She considered her childish remedy for insomnia but felt quite sure that counting sheep would be useless. The time differential caused her wakefulness; flying to another continent was bound to make her feel disoriented for a day or two. Just for fun she'd see whether there was a light under Felicia's door. If her roommate should be reading she'd creep in quietly and they could talk.

Gingerly she slipped out of bed and felt her way to the heavy wood door, opening it quietly. But the hall was as dark as the night, and no sliver of light invited her into the room opposite.

With a mental shrug Dizzy closed her own door once again, started back across the room and stubbed her toe on the protruding leg of a chair, whispering a sibilant "Ouch!" as she hobbled toward the bed. Then, as a single, high-pitched shriek came from somewhere beyond the garden, she froze where she stood. It was a cry of such pain and terror that it chilled her to the bone.

Stifled in mid course, the cry was not repeated, and Dizzy couldn't imagine what dire happening could have caused this outburst so close to the garden wall. Once more she huddled under the covers, listening anxiously, but only the weird, wild barking of a pack of dogs in the distance could be heard. Nearby, not even a cricket or a frog disturbed the recovered peace.

Three

"They're pariah dogs," Felicia told Dizzy the next morning. "Most Moroccans can't afford to keep pets the way Americans do, and the dogs become outcast and take to the desert or the mountains, where they grow wild and as mean as wolves. You probably heard one of them howl close at hand, that's all."

Dizzy didn't argue the point but she was certain that the shriek of agony had been human. No dog could make a sound like that. Still, the mind could play strange tricks in the middle of the night, and she didn't want to appear stubborn.

The girls were waiting for Rick to bring the car around and take them on a sight-seeing tour of the city. "We'll stop by the Bahia Palace and the Saadian Tombs and save the souks for tomorrow, when we can get going early," he said as they started off.

"Early? I call this early for vacation time." Felicia glanced at the hands of her wristwatch, which stood at ten thirty.

Aside from muttering, "Born lazy," Rick ignored his sister. He was busy avoiding half a dozen children playing in the road. "Do you realize," he asked Dizzy, "that of twelve million Moroccans almost half are under twenty? At this rate the population will have doubled in forty years."

"Rick's taking sociology at college," Felicia murmured. "If you aren't careful, Diz, he'll bore you to death with figures. Casablanca has a million inhabitants; there are more than a thousand Berber dialects; Moroccan illiteracy is frightening! What statistics would you like?"

"Shut up, Sis," said Rick cheerfully. "Where would you girls like to go first?"

"The palace," replied Dizzy at once, "and I want to know all about it, so don't let Felicia give you a complex. I'm interested."

She proved it by asking one question after another as Rick led them through the sumptuous Moorish-style reception rooms and courtyards built for a sultan's grand vizier. Fountains played and sunlight glinted on ornately painted double doors and was reflected to ceilings thirty feet high. The harem in particular fascinated Dizzy, and she wondered what it would have been like to be one of a bevy of veiled women peeking through the grilled windows at masculine gatherings below. Instinctively she shuddered. How dreadful to live in a society where a woman was considered a chattel. "What about Moroccans today?" she asked

Rick. "Is a man allowed to have more than one wife?"

"There's no law against it," Rick replied. "But only the very rich can afford it. Pop knows a phosphate millionaire who has four, but it's pretty expensive, maintaining that many different houses. There are no harems anymore, you see, because the Moroccans have finally found out that two women under the same roof fight like alley cats."

" 'One lamp cannot light two houses,' " quoted Felicia, who was always ready with literary allusions. "Old Chinese proverb applies here."

The Saadian tombs, where several sultans and other members of ruling families were buried, stood in three cedarwood-ceilinged halls in the midst of a beautiful garden, where bougainvillea was a riot of purples and pinks on the walls, and veiled nursemaids squatted on the ground gossiping while their charges played nearby. Bees buzzed among the flowers and a blind beggar, wrapped in a ragged jellaba, sat in the shade near the gate, causing Dizzy to search in her wallet for some money.

"Oh, dear," she said, finding only American change. "I must get a traveler's check cashed. Could we stop at a bank, Rick, on the way home?"

Dropping a coin into the beggar's hand, Rick groaned and suggested, "Let's put that off 'til tomorrow. It's almost noon, and it's a real operation, prying money loose from a Moroccan bank."

This seemed curious to Dizzy, who thought American checks should be welcomed anywhere. "Aren't you exaggerating?" she asked in mild annoyance. "Why don't you just say it's hot and you'd rather get along home?"

The moment she had spoken she was sorry, because Rick shook his head in surprise. Just because he was putting off a dull errand was no reason to scold. "Never mind," she said more gently. "One day's as good as another, actually."

Back at the house there was a flurry of activity. A Land Rover and a ten-year-old Chevrolet nudged each other in the drive, where Dr. Harding was directing the loading of a miscellaneous assortment of baggage.

There were wooden crates and metal boxes marked "Explosives," tools and what appeared to be scientific instruments, duffel bags and tents, all of which were being stowed in an order that would fit them into the limited space. Ali and an old gardener called Abdul were struggling to lift the heavy gear into the rear of the Land Rover where Bou Hamida was stationed, bent double as he packed each piece in the position designated. Dr. Harding had a list in one hand and a pencil in the other, so that each item loaded could systematically be checked off. He called a cheerful hello to the girls, said, "Patrick, I could use you here for a while," and turned to indicate a bundle of folding canvas cots. "These should go next, Ali, right on top of the tent."

The sun was almost directly overhead, hot and relentless. "Gosh," Dizzy heard Rick complain. "What's all the hurry, Pop? Don't tell me you plan to leave today?"

His father nodded. "No need to hang around, now that Dr. Hazziz has given us the go-ahead. If we get off by four we should be able to cross the Tizi N' Tichka Pass and be in Ouarzazate by dark."

The foreign names sounded strange to Dizzy, and somehow ominous. She followed Felicia into the house and walked through the hall to the long doors leading out to the garden, where she peered through the trees toward the High Atlas, but the brooding mountains had disappeared in the heat haze. Ridiculously, she was filled with a sense of foreboding, and wondered at the adventurousness of men like Dr. Harding, who was apparently at home in so many different environments–his classroom at M.I.T., this elegantly appointed house, and prospecting in the vast uncharted desert beyond the mountains.

"What's the matter?" Felicia asked at Dizzy's shoulder. "What are you daydreaming about?"

"Your father. I should think it would be scary, going off with an Arab crew on a trip like that. Why all the explosives? Aren't they dangerous?"

Felicia looked surprised. "He's used to field work,

and the men are hand picked. They use the dynamite to set off small explosions called ground shots, and the scientific instruments detect the shock waves they send through the sand and rocks."

"Rocks? In the desert?" Dizzy's inflection showed her surprise.

Felicia nodded. "There are stony deserts as well as sand deserts in Morocco, you know."

Dizzy hadn't known, but she tried to look intelligent as she nodded. "Go on."

"The next step is more complicated," Felicia admitted. "I don't quite understand it myself, but Father says they look for possible reflections of these vibrations from pools of oil deep underground. This part must be exciting, and I think Dad's looking forward to some action. It's hard for a vigorous man like him to be tied to a desk day in and day out."

"How long will he be gone?"

Felicia shrugged. "A week, two weeks. It depends on how soon they locate oil. I suppose it could be nearly a month."

"But you think they really will find it?"

"Oil? Of course, if Father says so. I've never known him to go off on a wild goose chase."

Felicia's confidence in her father was obviously shared by the rest of the family. At lunch, served on trays in the garden under the shade of spreading date palms, everyone talked about the prospecting trip to the desert as though the successful outcome of the mission on which Dr. Harding was setting forth was a virtual certainty.

Only Dizzy continued to feel some uneasiness, which a glimpse of the headlines in *Le Petit Marocain* did nothing to allay. "Russians Drill for Oil near Algerian Border," she read and couldn't help but feel that the Soviets were getting uncomfortably close. Suppose the two teams should meet at this frontier, which she could only envision as an imaginary line running across a sandy wasteland? With the reputation both the Russians and the Algerians had for belligerence, mightn't Dr. Harding be in some danger? She didn't voice such questions, but she was surprised at the casual manner in which the family prepared to see the head of the household off. If it were *her* father packing the Land Rover and preparing to camp in the desert with a bunch of mysterious-looking Arabs, she wouldn't like it one bit.

After lunch everyone retired for the usual siesta and the house was quiet until nearly four, when sounds of activity roused Dizzy and brought her downstairs to find Rick sitting in the hall cleaning a gun. He pushed wadding through the barrel carefully, then squinted down the shiny length of metal tubing he had pointed toward the light.

"Goodness, that looks lethal," commented Dizzy. Her own father didn't own a gun, and was opposed to any kind of hunting. The Driscolls always fed the pheasants in the winter and shuddered at the sight of dead deer being car-hauled from New England during the fall hunting season. Dizzy naturally shared their distaste.

She was, however, far more adventurous than either of her parents, or she wouldn't have come to Marrakech when the opportunity presented itself. And now that she was here she was determined to become acclimated to the new environment as quickly as possible. If Morocco meant guns and desert safaris and strange sounds in the night she'd better stifle her misgivings and emulate Felicia's tranquillity.

"You about through, Patrick? I'm ready to leave," called Dr. Harding, hurrying downstairs ahead of his wife.

"Two secs," Rick returned, and knelt on the marble floor to fit the gun and cleaning equipment into a case. Outside two Berber workmen in desert gear stood by the Land Rover and Bou Hamida was emerging from the Chevrolet with a briefcase in his hand. He turned it over at once to his chief, who thanked him briskly.

"We're all set to go. I'll reach Ouarzazate tonight and Tinerhir tomorrow. You'll have your two technicians ready to leave first thing in the morning, and you'll drive straight through. Right?"

"Right," agreed the Arab, bowing slightly.

Dr. Harding held out his hand. "Good-bye, then.

Better get off early, in case of a breakdown. I'll arrange to hire the jeep and have it stocked with supplies for the desert. That's one of the reasons I'm going on ahead."

"Yes, sir."

"So I'll see you tomorrow night."

"*Inch' Allah*," replied Bou Hamida.

"You *be* there," Dr. Harding said in a tone that brooked no argument.

Dizzy, standing at one side with Rick and Felicia, asked softly, "What does '*Inch' Allah*' mean?"

"If God wills," replied Felicia. "All the Muslims say it but it always annoys Father. I don't know why."

"I do," said Rick with a chuckle. "It implies an authority other than his own. When Pop gives an order he expects to have it obeyed, whether Allah likes it or not."

"Sh," cautioned Felicia. "Bou Hamida will think you're sacrilegious."

"He can't hear me," Rick whispered back, but at that moment Dr. Harding's assistant turned and glanced toward the young people. An expression of contempt crossed his face. At once it was succeeded by a smile, and he came over and spoke to them courteously, but, fleeting as it was, Dizzy was sure the contempt had been there.

"Take care of your mother while I'm gone," Dr. Harding was now saying to Rick. He kissed Felicia affectionately, shook Dizzy's hand, then turned to embrace his wife. "If your sister comes on from Paris tell her I'm sorry to have missed her. Maybe you can persuade her to stay until I get back."

"I'll try," promised Mrs. Harding. "But you know Janet. When she's abroad she races from place to place as though it was her last chance to see the world."

Dr. Harding grinned. "Well, give her my love, anyway. And take care, darling."

"*You* take care, Patrick dear."

"Sure thing. I always do."

There was a chorus of good-byes to which Louella's Southern contralto added a grace note. She had arrived at the last moment bearing a paper bag in her hand. "Oatmeal cookies," she announced as she handed it ceremoniously to Dr. Harding. "You can get mighty hungry in the mountains, I hear tell."

A moment later the Land Rover roared through the gate, followed more sedately by the Chevrolet on its return trip to the office, and the courtyard was suddenly quiet. Mrs. Harding sighed and turned toward the house. "I hope he remembers to wear his helmet," she said to everyone and no one. "I always worry about sunstroke when he goes South."

"Stay cool, Mother. Pop's a big boy now," Rick teased.

Although Mrs. Harding said compulsively, "I do wish, Patrick, that you would not use that vulgar term for your father," she seemed to relax and went back into the house humming a tune under her breath.

Felicia, who had carried a book downstairs, headed for the sofa in the library, but Dizzy and Rick loitered outside near the lily pools, where a pair of turtles were sunning on the rim.

"They must be Moroccan turtles," Dizzy said. "Look, they're gray instead of brown and they're almost twice the size of ours at home."

Rick poked at one with a twig, and instead of retiring into its shell the creature turned to stare at the young man contemptuously. At this Dizzy burst out laughing. "He looks just like Bou Hamida! Oh, Rick, isn't that funny? He really does."

"You must be seeing things," said Rick skeptically. "He looks about as much like Bou Hamida as I do." Squelched, Dizzy didn't try to explain that it was not the physiognomy but the expression of the turtle and the Arab that she was comparing. She had made herself a promise that she wouldn't fall into the habit of arguing needlessly with Felicia's brother. Since she was going to live under the same roof with him for some weeks, it behooved her to stay cool and collected.

"Now if you had said our peacock looks like the Countess I'd have gone along," Rick was musing. He indicated the brilliantly feathered bird stepping along a gravel path between two flower beds. "There's a certain way of carrying the neck—"

Dizzy grinned, instantly mollified. "Rick, you're a clown, just as Felicia said."

"My sister said that? Well, I'll have you know she's maligning me. I'm a very serious type, actually, apt to become a sterling citizen and a fine businessman, if I ever grow up."

Dizzy found it impossible not to be amused by Rick's nonsense. She walked around the house with him to the garden terrace and stretched out in the shade, where they chatted idly until the sun at last started to drop behind the trees.

"O.K. Time to be off and running," the boy said as though this were a signal. He jumped to his feet and tapped on the library window. "Come on, Sis! Let's show Dizzy the Djemaa-el-Fna."

Felicia, lying supine with her long legs stretched over one arm of the sofa, glanced up from her book languidly. "You show her," she proposed. "I'm just at the most exciting part."

How the printed word could possibly compare with the joy of doing things Dizzy couldn't understand, but she had grown accustomed to her roommate's temperament and she wasn't in the least surprised that Rick's urging met with no success.

In the end the pair went off together, telling Mrs. Harding where they were headed and promising to be back by dark. Rick had raided his mother's purse for all her loose change, which jingled in the pocket of his slacks as he ran to get the car. "It's customary to give the entertainers a little something," he explained on the way to the center of the city, "and small coins are about the hardest thing to come by in Marrakech."

By now Dizzy had learned that a dirham, which looked a good deal like an American quarter, was the medium of exchange, and that at five dirhams (roughly the equivalent of a United States dollar) paper money began to appear. The ten, twenty, and fifty franc coppers into which the dirham was divided she had not yet tried to master, but it was these that everyone seemed to need constantly. She *must* remember to go to the bank tomorrow, but this afternoon there were more exciting things to do.

The Djemaa-el-Fna was less than a mile from the house, so the drive was short. As Rick parked the car at the edge of the great square he said with a chuckle, "The name's supposed to mean the Assembly of the Dead, but it doesn't look dead now, does it?"

With thousands of people milling around the huge, rather vague triangle which was actually no square at all, its character had completely changed from that hastily glimpsed on the previous afternoon. "It's like a ten ring circus," Dizzy murmured as she followed Rick into the colorful maelstrom.

"Or an enormous theater where you can choose your entertainment to suit your taste." Rick took Dizzy's hand and pulled her into a circle of spectators, several of whom were tourists carrying cameras. "Look. Here's a snake charmer."

Dizzy stood on tiptoe to peer over the shoulder of a heavily veiled Arab woman carrying a baby in a sling on her back. In a cleared space stood a bushy-haired, black-eyed man in filthy white robes lifting a huge hooded cobra from a wicker basket at his feet. He was shouting for the audience's attention as he held the great snake in his outstretched hand, allowed it to twist around his neck, and then as a climax to the routine tucked it into his open shirt against his bare chest.

Instinctively shuddering, Dizzy shrank back and said, "Ugh," but her companion merely grinned. "Take a closer look," he advised. "Both the snake and his master are very blasé. The snake's fangs have been pulled, and he's quite harmless. It's all in the day's work."

After tossing a coin to the carpet that served as a stage, Rick led Dizzy on to a pair of mischievous monkeys and their trainer who were performing for a crowd of children, then in turn to a sword-swallower, a fire-eater and a storyteller, the last of whom was attracting the biggest crowd of all.

"What sort of stories is he telling?" Dizzy asked Rick as she watched the spellbound faces. "Is he giving them the news?"

Rick shook his head. "He tells very old stories, usually, from Moroccan folklore that has come down through many generations by word of mouth. You have to remember that not many of these people can read or write. They have no television and only the lucky few have transistor radios. Storytellers furnish the entertainment poor people don't get in other ways."

Dizzy and Rick wandered on, past scribes sitting on the ground before their writing boxes, waiting for customers. The two paused briefly before a group of Negro dancers (from Mauritania, Rick said) gyrating to the rhythmic beat of an instrument called a *tam-tam*. Nearby, acrobats from the mountain village of Amizmiz performed such amazing feats that they drew a roar of approval from the spectators as a shower of coins fell at their feet. Skirting a crowd around a pair of fighting cocks, Rick led Dizzy on toward the center of the melee, in search of some Berber dancers he claimed to be the best of all. He sidestepped a donkey driver shouting "*Balek! Balek!*" and suddenly came face to face with the Countess de Redier and Bou Hamida, who were apparently coming from the souks, since both carried packages.

The Countess greeted the young people with apparent pleasure. After inquiring whether Dizzy was enjoying the carnival, she said, "I never tire of coming here. There are always new faces and new sights. Somehow the Djemaa-el-Fna still seems like a huge stopover for caravans, a place where mountain and desert people meet or pass through." Then she asked, "Where's Felicia? Is she ill?"

"Oh, no," Dizzy said. "She's reading."

"Which reminds me that I have some paperbacks to pass on to her," said the Countess. "I'll try to stop by—"

"We could pick them up tomorrow morning on our way to the souks," Rick suggested when she hesitated. "That is if it would be convenient. We'll be starting out about nine o'clock."

"Splendid!" replied the Countess. "Usually I don't leave for the office until nearly nine thirty." She added, politely, "Bou Hamida tells me that your father got off on time."

Rick nodded. "Right on schedule, as usual, with a bag of Louella's cookies in his hand."

The Countess smiled. "Dear Louella. She really loves him."

"She loves all of us," Rick replied quite seriously, "and we love her."

"Your family is very fortunate," said Bou Hamida with his usual formality, "to have such a loyal servant."

As they turned away Dizzy mused on how little Dr. Harding's assistant seemed to understand the relationship which really existed between a person like Louella and the family she worked for. Over here the class system was still positively medieval. She doubted if Bou Hamida even knew the names of the Arab helpers in the Harding household, although he must have come there often. Certainly he treated Ali and Abdul as though they were part of the landscape rather than as individuals.

Twilight was falling now, and the long wailing song of the muezzins was attracting the faithful away from the diversions of the square toward the mosques. In the souks to the north the pale acetylene lights of the more persistent merchants were flickering, but most of the tourists were drifting toward the taxi stands or carriages.

"Buggy-buggy, Miss?" asked an old fellow standing by his horse.

Dizzy shook her head. "No, thank you." She smiled at the man and he grinned back. "American," he announced sagely to the evening air.

"To Americans the drivers usually say 'buggy-buggy,' to the French and English '*calèche*,'" Rick told her as they approached the car. "As soon as they get to recognize you they won't try to overcharge you, but in the beginning watch out. It's best to arrive at a price before you get in."

Dizzy listened carefully. It intrigued her to think that she might travel around Marrakech alone, and she wanted to seem sophisticated rather than gauche.

Back at the house the ground floor rooms were all lighted, and as soon as Dizzy and Rick entered the hall they sensed an atmosphere of strain. Through the library door they could see Mrs. Harding at the telephone. She was repeating "*Allo! Allo!*" in the high-pitched French manner used to contact the operator, and her daughter was hovering by her shoulder as though something were gravely amiss.

At the sound of footfalls on the marble floor Felicia turned and hurried to her brother. "Mother's in a tizzy," she said in a stage whisper. "Aunt Janet's got to go to a Paris hospital for an emergency operation, and of course Mother insists on being with her. She's trying to get reservations on tomorrow morning's plane."

"Is it serious? The operation, I mean?" Rick asked.

"Serious enough, I guess."

At that moment Mrs. Harding hung up. "There's no use trying to get the desk at the ticket office," she complained in annoyance. "They only answer when they feel like it."

"I could run downtown in the car," Rick proposed quickly, while Dizzy noted that in an emergency he discarded his playful-puppy attitude and acquired some of his father's efficiency.

"A good idea, Patrick," said Mrs. Harding at once. "It shouldn't take you more than half an hour. I'll have Louella hold dinner until you get back."

"What sort of space do you want?"

"Anything I can get. There's only one plane direct to Paris all week and it may be crowded. Explain that it's an emergency."

"Shall do," Rick called back as he hurried off.

Four

Mrs. Harding was distraught. There was no doubt about it. Her usual composure, although not shattered, was certainly chipped.

When Dizzy came downstairs after changing for dinner she found her hostess pacing up and down the living room while Felicia perched on the arm of a chair, regarding her mother helplessly. "I can't imagine what can be keeping that child," Mrs. Harding was saying. "The airline office closes like the grave at eight o'clock and it's already twenty past."

"Don't worry, Mother; he'll be along in a minute," Felicia said soothingly, but Mrs. Harding was not comforted. "I simply must get on that plane. I know what I'll do! I'll phone Philip Goodhue." At once she started for the library.

"Who's Philip Goodhue?" inquired Dizzy when she and Felicia were alone.

"He's head of the *Maison de l'Amerique*—a good

friend of Mother's and Father's, and he certainly ought to have some influence with the airline, wouldn't you think?"

It was a rhetorical question. Dizzy could see that Felicia was nearly as upset as Mrs. Harding by this unexpected turn of events. "Aunt Janet's such a doll," she told Dizzy. "She's ten years younger than Mother, and after our grandmother died Mother practically raised her. In spite of the difference in age they've always been very close."

At that moment Rick came hurrying into the house and Mrs. Harding abandoned the telephone, where she had been getting a busy signal. "You're all set," Rick announced cheerfully. "It took Mr. Goodhue to arrange it, but you've got a first class reservation and he'll stop by for you with his driver at eight o'clock sharp. You see, by coincidence, he's taking the same plane."

Mrs. Harding and Felicia both seemed astonished that Rick had gone direct from the airline office to Mr. Goodhue. Over dinner they congratulated him for his aggressiveness and he basked under their approval. "You know what Pop says: always go to the top."

Dizzy munched on a piece of roll to keep from smiling as she steeled herself for the inevitable, "I do wish, Patrick—" but Mrs. Harding stifled her routine criticism. "I'm glad Philip happens to be going to Paris too," she said instead. "It will be nice to have company on the flight."

When Ali brought mint tea to the terrace as usual, Louella followed him, sailing along in her white kitchen apron like a sloop in a gentle breeze. "Please sit down," her mistress suggested, then quickly described the emergency that called her away. "I'll leave you in charge of the children and the kitchen. Ali can take care of the rest of the staff. Hopefully, I'll be back within a week."

"You don't worry about a thing, Mrs. Harding. I can even manage those Ayrabs if I have to. They understand my sign language real good."

Rick chuckled. "Besides, we're not exactly children anymore, Mother. We'll be fine."

Due to the Moroccan custom of serving breakfast in the bedrooms rather than downstairs, it was arranged that Mrs. Harding say her good-byes that evening so that she could leave the next morning with a minimum of confusion. "Aunt Janet says Paris is terribly crowded, but she'll get me into a hotel somewhere and try to call back tonight." She turned to Felicia, whom she apparently considered the more responsible of her children. "I'll leave the addresses of my hotel and the hospital under the flower bowl on the hall table," she said as they went upstairs.

To Dizzy her hostess said a rather apologetic farewell. "I hate to run out on you this way, Deborah, but you'll be in competent hands with Louella. Besides, in an emergency—heaven forbid!—there's always the telephone."

From the way the telephone had been behaving this evening Dizzy didn't put much faith in it, but if its presence in the house comforted Mrs. Harding it was all to the good. As she undressed for bed, Dizzy listened for the promised call from Paris, but when she fell asleep it had not yet come.

The next thing she knew it was broad daylight and birds were cheeping on her balcony. There was one that made a sound for all the world like the snap of a metal cricket a hundred times magnified. Trying to imitate the sharp call, Dizzy clicked her tongue against the roof of her mouth, and for a few seconds the bird stopped and listened, then continued its raucous cheep more stridently than before.

Louella herself brought Dizzy's breakfast tray, with the air of a junior executive in a new and responsible job. She said a soft good morning, announced that Mrs. Harding had already left, remarked that Patrick had come down to see his mother off, and remembered she was to tell the girls he'd be ready to leave for the medina by nine o'clock.

Dizzy was always running into new Moroccan words. "What's the medina, Louella? I thought we were going to the souks."

"The medina's where the souks *is*," Louella replied. "You might as well say the market district's where the shops *is*. Takes a while to get on to all these foreign names."

Dizzy smiled. "Pretty soon you'll be speaking Arabic."

"Not me," Louella said firmly. "Now I gotta go get Felicia roused, and that ain't easy."

Nevertheless, Felicia appeared downstairs no more than five minutes late and seemed pleased to be going to the souks. She was wearing a cotton-knit dress and had a sweater flung over her shoulders.

"You won't need that, Sis," Rick said as she got into the car, but it was too much trouble to take the sweater back to the house, so Felicia stuffed it into the straw basket she was carrying. She had the reputation at Abbott Academy of toting the most books and the greatest amount of hand luggage of anyone in school. "Felicia leaves for her morning classes with enough stuff to take her to Timbuktu and back," a classmate had once commented, and Dizzy was forced to agree.

Today, besides the sweater, she was carrying sun glasses, a crushable cotton hat, the book she was currently reading, a bottle of aspirin, several packets of Wash n' Dri, a guide to Marrakech that she thought might interest Dizzy, a package of Kleenex, a small transistor radio, a large pink plastic comb, and a bottle of French toilet water acquired on the plane from Paris at a discount price. "I'll sort it out tomorrow," she said as she rummaged through the basket for the guidebook. In the meantime she was prepared to haul it all along without complaint.

It was Dizzy who remembered they were to stop at the Countess de Redier's apartment for the books she had promised to lend to Felicia. The Countess lived within a short distance of the Koutoubia, in a charming gray plaster house converted into small flats. She waved to the young people from a window on the second floor, and called to Felicia, who had climbed out of the car to collect her booty, "Don't come up. I'll be right down."

Dressed in a simple sleeveless linen, the Countess looked younger this morning than she had at the dinner party. Hurrying up to Felicia, she handed her half a dozen paperbacks, waved away her thanks, then turned to Rick, who had courteously emerged from the driver's seat.

"I've got a problem," she confessed. "One of your father's prospecting team, a young Berber named Ibrahim, who speaks a little English, apparently misunderstood his instructions and has gone back home to Amizmiz. Bou Hamida just called and sounded quite upset. He can't seem to reach the village by phone, so he'd like us to drive out and try to bring Ibrahim back to Marrakech in time to leave with the rest of the expedition. Do you think the girls could spare you for the morning, Patrick?"

"Of course," Rick said at once. "If they get lost in the souks they can always hire a small boy to lead them back to civilization. How far is Amizmiz from here?"

"Only about fifty kilometers," replied the Countess. "It's a hamlet in the mountains out past the Casbah of Oumnast and the Cavagnac Dam. With luck we should be back by noon."

Felicia, who had been tucking the new books into her already bulging basket, glanced at her wristwatch. "You'd better get started," she suggested practically. "Dizzy and I can walk from here."

However, Rick insisted on driving the girls as far as the Bab Agnou Gate, set in the red city ramparts like a jewel in a crown. As the car stopped in a flurry of dust Dizzy asked, "Isn't Amizmiz the village the acrobats come from?" She was recalling the human pyramid glimpsed briefly last evening in the Djemaa-el-Fna.

The Countess, now ensconced in the front seat next to the driver, nodded. "For generations dozens of young men trained in that one small village have gone off to Europe and America as circus performers. This, of course, explains Ibrahim's smattering of English." She added, "His grandfather was a famous acrobat who worked in both London and New York."

Impatient to be off, Rick turned the car into the roadway once more, calling good-bye and narrowly escaping a donkey driver, who cried "*Balek, Bal-e-e-e-k!*"

in a warning treble. Dizzy stepped back to let him pass her in the gateway, then stayed close to Felicia's side as they entered a maze of small streets crowded with Arabs buying and selling, working and loafing, talking and laughing, cooking, eating, pursuing the myriad occupations that made up their daily lives.

Jogging along with the raw materials of Moroccan commerce came the porters, their backs piled high with bundles of tanned leather, bales of sheep's wool, bags of spices. A few late-rising merchants were still taking off the heavy wooden shutters that protected their shops, and less affluent businessmen were squatting in front of trays of gimcrackery ranging from cheap, shiny jewelry to garishly colored portraits of the King.

In row upon row of one-room factories scarcely bigger than American coat closets artisans had been busy since dawn. Tailors were sewing on jellabas by hand while holding the thread with their toes. Coppersmiths were hammering intricate designs on trays and teapots. Children or old men were painting black patterns on pottery, using their fingers as brushes. Shoemakers were spitting out nails with which to tack leather heels on the pointed Turkish slippers called *babouches*, in which most Moroccans slip-slapped around the streets. Dizzy stopped again and again, fascinated. "Oh, Felicia, look at this! And this. And this."

Her roommate was indulgent but not so enthralled

at watching a barber scalping a tiny child of all but the single lock of hair needed to pull him into paradise. Nor, she confessed, did copper and brass displays seem so tempting as they had last year. But in the wool souks Felicia was as captivated as Dizzy by the bright skeins hanging from latticelike awnings that threw stripes of sunlight on the throng beneath. Red, green, blue, yellow, cerise, the wool was still wet from the dyers' vats but almost ready for the process of transformation into intricately patterned rugs.

By now the girls, who had managed to avoid the importunities of half a dozen hopeful guides, had acquired a cortege of small boys, each of whom had a few words of English and a special souk to which he attempted to draw the young Americans.

"*Allah ihennik*," Felicia kept saying firmly, using the Arabic good-bye. After a while most of the children went off to seek more cooperative tourists, but one especially persistent youngster kept picking at Dizzy's skirt and asking, "You buy caftan? Good caftan?"

"As a matter of fact," Dizzy said to Felicia, "I *would* like to look at caftans. Mother wants me to try to find one she can wear as an evening coat." Smiling down at the urchin, she asked, "Where?"

"*Qrib*," he replied, running ahead happily while Felicia translated another Arabic expression she had learned to recognize. "He says it's quite near."

This, however, proved to be an exaggeration. The

girls were led along a dark alley to the right of the wool souks, then through another long lane of shops where the sun filtered through a reed canopy as if through a stained-glass window. Skipping ahead, then running back to make sure they still were following, the boy took his amused captives through a maze of narrow streets with so many turnings that Dizzy became utterly confused. "I wonder if *he* knows where he's going?" she asked.

Felicia shrugged. "I certainly don't," she admitted, "but then I often get lost in the medina. And as Rick says, for a dirham there's always another small boy happy to show you the way out."

Ahead, the lad had stopped to talk to a donkey driver who looked vaguely familiar to Dizzy. "Isn't that the same fellow Rick almost ran down back at the gate?" she asked.

Felicia glanced at the grizzled face under a carelessly wrapped turban. "I rather doubt it," she replied. "They all look alike."

Now they had entered a more prosperous section, where tourist goods were displayed. The souks were bigger here, with narrow entryways leading to large electrically lighted rooms stacked to the ceiling with rugs or filled with camel seats, hassocks, and leather goods of all descriptions.

In front of an entry lined with glass cases the boy stopped short. "*Hena!*" he said. "Here." To the proprietor he spoke in Arabic, proudly, and as the girls were ushered unctuously into the back room he was sent off with a couple of coins in his hand.

"You want to see caftans?" asked the plump Arab into whose charge they had been given. He spoke to Dizzy, so the child had apparently designated her as the potential customer. "How much you want to pay?"

"How much are they?" asked Dizzy, who was unaccustomed to Moroccan bargaining and who had also taken an unreasonable dislike to the man's fawning manner.

The storekeeper shrugged but continued to smile speciously. "All prices. You like new caftan? Very cheap."

"I think she'd like to see some antique caftans," suggested Felicia. Then she said to Dizzy, "The material in the new ones is pretty shoddy, but if you can find one that will fit, the old ones are often perfectly beautiful."

"Antique caftans very rare, very expensive," the merchant said as he stepped across a pile of rugs to a row of shelves stacked neatly with folded robes. He considered for a moment, then pulled out a black silk caftan heavily embroidered in gold thread. This garment he spread out on a counter. "You like?"

"It's very pretty," Dizzy replied. "How much is it?"

"How much you want to pay?"

Oh, dear, thought Dizzy, here we go again. She

hadn't the slightest idea what the caftan was worth, so she sidestepped the question. "Could we see some others?" she asked instead.

"*Mais oui*," said the merchant. "You see all, you try on, then decide."

"It isn't for me," Dizzy hastened to explain. "It's for my mother."

"Ah!" The man turned from rummaging through the robes. "*Elle est petite, comme ça?*" He apparently had lapsed into French, a language in which he felt more at home than English, without thinking.

Dizzy shook her head, because her mother was closer to Felicia's height than her own. "*Plus grande*," she said, indicating her roommate. "*Comme ça*."

This the Arab seemed to find extremely amusing. He began to display one caftan after another, as quickly as he could get them down from the shelves. "*Pour La Petite*," he would cry, or "*pour La Grande*," depending on whether they were small or large. Obviously he considered himself a clever fellow to have settled on these quite obvious nicknames for his customers.

"I don't know how I got drawn into this thing," Felicia complained, but any of the caftans in which Dizzy seemed interested she agreeably tried on. One, in dark green silk embroidered with a design of golden birds, was particularly handsome.

"The very finest," declared the merchant, ready to

praise any item that met with the girls' approval. "Pure gold thread, see?"

It certainly looked like gold to Dizzy, although she was no expert in such matters. However, anything that looked this becoming on Felicia would certainly suit her mother, whose hair was a slightly darker blond.

"How much?" she assayed once more.

This time the storekeeper seemed to be making ready to reply. With the air of a fisherman who has hooked his fish but must proceed to net it he sent Felicia to the door to examine the quality of the garment in daylight. "For *La Petite*," he then whispered conspiratorially to Dizzy, "I make a very special price. One hundred dollars."

"One hundred dollars!" Dizzy's cry of alarm was genuine. "I'm sorry, but I couldn't possibly afford it."

"How much you want to pay?" the Arab asked, not unexpectedly.

Dizzy shook her head, unwilling to admit that her mother had mentioned a top figure of fifty dollars, so the dealer attempted another ploy. From a wrapping of white paper, a protection not accorded the other merchandise, he took a cream-colored caftan so thickly embroidered in gold that it could almost stand alone, and so gorgeous that Dizzy gasped.

"Very small size, for a little princess," the storekeeper said, and held it up for her to try on.

"Oh, no." Dizzy backed away, although she was sorely tempted. "It's heavenly, but I couldn't, really—"

"No charge for trying," the Arab purred, and somehow Dizzy found herself standing in front of a long mirror in the beautiful garment, which could indeed have been made for a princess of the royal harem, it was so finely sewn.

At this moment Felicia came back into the room, still blinking from her foray into the daylight and with a curious expression on her face. Dizzy expected an immediate reaction to her appearance in the magnificent caftan, but instead her roommate seemed unimpressed.

"The most peculiar thing," she murmured. "I've simply got to tell you. . . ." Then she bit her lip as she noticed the Arab regarding her closely in the mirror before which both girls now stood.

At that moment a diversion was created by the entry of the boy who had acted as their self-appointed guide. He was carrying a brass tray set with a teapot and three glasses, which he put down on a low table with an air of having carried out a commission successfully.

"You like a glass of mint tea, please," said the storekeeper as the urchin disappeared once more.

Felicia nodded and said, "*Merci beaucoup,*" so Dizzy followed suit. She remembered having been told that it was very discourteous *ever* to refuse refreshments offered by a Moroccan, yet she felt uncomfortable, because she suspected this was but a prelude to a serious bargaining session for which she was unprepared.

Besides, Felicia's unfinished remark had aroused her curiosity. What could her roommate have seen to startle her out of her usual equanimity? Even now she stood sipping the tea and frowning as though she were deeply disturbed.

Both girls were still wearing the heavy caftans over their dresses, and suddenly Dizzy began to feel faint. Between the steaming tea and the weight of the gold-encrusted garment such a reaction was predictable, but still it rather surprised her. She had never been subject to spells of vertigo.

Conflicting desires surged through her. Anxious only to be finished and away—the caftan bargaining could surely wait for another day!—she began to gulp the sweet hot liquid hastily, at the same time trying to shrug off the heavy caftan so she could be cooler. Felicia, although she must have been equally uncomfortable, seemed to be standing by in a daze. Her eyes were fixed on the mirror, which reflected a vertical section of the street outside, and she was sipping her mint tea abstractedly.

"I'm not—not feeling very well," Dizzy heard herself saying, and she realized with dismay that she had let the precious caftan fall to the rug-strewn floor. In an effort to put her empty glass back on the tray she took a couple of tottering steps forward.

"Sit down and put your head between your knees," she heard Felicia advise as though from a long distance. Helpless to obey, she felt herself falling, and then the world turned completely black.

Five

Dizzy returned to consciousness slowly and painfully. She was aware of a splitting headache and a strange taste in her mouth, and felt as though she were whirling through an endless tunnel. There was no beginning and no end.

Tentatively she opened her eyes, then closed them again and tried to collect her wits. She must have fainted. What an absurd, Victorian thing to have done! How embarrassing for Felicia, to say nothing of her own humiliation. Breathing deeply, she made a determined effort to pull herself together and opened her eyes once more.

This time she kept them open long enough to become aware that the scene had changed. She was no longer in the high-ceilinged room with the shelves piled with caftans, the long mirror and the tray of glasses and pot of mint tea. She was lying on a pile of dusty rugs in what must be a small storeroom, and she was quite alone.

This, in itself, was curious. Where was Felicia? What had become of the Arab merchant? A thrill of fear swept through her. So Marrakech was a city where everyone was kindly and honest, where a couple of girls could feel safe and secure wherever they went. Indeed!

Wetting her dry lips with the tip of her tongue, Dizzy noticed the bitter taste once again, almost obscuring the lingering savor of sweet mint tea. The pounding in her head began to lessen, so that she could think a little more clearly. Putting two and two together came out to a logical four. The swoon wasn't due to the heat at all; she must have been given a drug, perhaps the sort mystery-story writers referred to as knockout drops.

Alarm now forced her to try to sit up, but she was still too dizzy to risk getting to her feet, so she remained propped on one elbow as she examined the room. Moroccan rugs were piled high in all four corners, leaving a cleared space in the middle scarcely larger than a king-sized bed. It was here that she was lying, on a folded carpet apparently pulled down from one of the stacks to serve as a makeshift pallet. At her feet was a closed door and behind her (heavens, how it hurt to turn her head!) another. Light filtered weakly under the sills and from a dirty overhead transom. The high, thick piles of rugs must be acting as a barrier to sound, because the quiet was intense.

Then a scratching noise made her start. A mouse?

No, it was the grating of a key in a lock. Instinctively playing for time, Dizzy fell back and shut her eyes once more, trying to breathe deeply and evenly as though she were still asleep.

The door opened, squeaking slightly, and someone entered the room, stood over her for several moments, then went out and locked the door carefully. It was infuriating not to have caught a glimpse of the visitor, but Dizzy felt sure that the flicker of an eyelash would have betrayed her and she dared not take the chance. Besides, from the heavy footfalls and the sound of breathing she felt certain that it was a man who had come and gone. Of course she couldn't be sure, but his identity was easy to guess—the oily Arab merchant who had cajoled her into trying on the caftan of the little princess, while Felicia had been lured into examining the green and gold garment in the street.

But Felicia had returned, Dizzy realized as her head began to clear and the aching ebbed away. Felicia had been urging her, just before she lost consciousness, "Sit down and put your head between your knees."

Where was Felicia now? Dizzy asked herself once again, and considered the possibilities. Her roommate might simply have gone for a doctor, but then why should she be locked in this back room? Besides, Felicia had drunk the mint tea too, not quite so fast, perhaps, but one could expect the same eventual results. Then where *was* Felicia—captive in another room? And why?

Why was the big and unanswerable question. Practical by nature, Dizzy therefore put it out of her mind and struggled to her feet. For a minute or two she felt tottery, but she forced herself to stay upright, even though she leaned for support against one of the stacks of rugs.

Then, gathering both strength and courage, she went over to the door through which her visitor had come, knelt on the floor and tried to peer through the keyhole, but she was rewarded by nothing but blackness. The key must have been left in place on the other side.

Anger gradually began to replace the terror Dizzy had felt when she had first regained consciousness. The more normal she became the more furious she got. How dared that fellow think he could trap and imprison two American girls? She'd go to the police, that's what she'd do, and report him, just as soon as she got out of here.

Without the slightest doubt that the opposite door would also be locked on the outside, Dizzy walked across the cleared space and tried the handle, which to her astonishment turned in her fingers. She opened the door a crack and found that it gave on the sort of narrow alley Rick called a *derb*.

Built between the walls of two crumbling buildings, the passageway was so cramped a burro might barely have squeezed through. Arches buttressed the walls on either side, and through cracks in these a few feeble rays of light managed to penetrate.

At the moment the *derb* was quite empty, but from a distance the muted roar of the medina fell on Dizzy's ears. To the left she could see a facing wall into which was set a tiled fountain and to the right, a hundred yards distant, was a narrow opening to a busy street.

Hesitating only a moment, during which she tried to locate herself relative to the souk where she had been shown the caftans, Dizzy ran swiftly down the alley toward the fountain, where three small boys were playing in the dirt. They glanced up at her curiously, but she dared not slow to a walk. It was imperative to put as much space as possible between herself and that wretched back room where she had been dumped like a sack of meal. Concerning Felicia's possible plight she was deeply troubled, but she was also aware that alone she was helpless. The only sensible course was to get clear of the place and go to the police.

But Dizzy had reckoned without the young Hardings' knowledge of the web of paths and corridors, covered arcades, dead-end passages, cul-de-sacs, and crooked lanes that make up the Marrakech medina. As she sped along one alley after another, twisting this way and that as opportunity presented itself, she lost all sense of direction and feared that she was fated to wander in this intricate maze forever. Then she remembered Rick's advice. A small boy will always show you the way home for a dirham. But where was her handbag? Suddenly Dizzy stopped short, clenching her teeth against the realization that until this moment she hadn't given her purse a thought.

Too late she realized how overwrought she had been, so frantic to get away that she had failed not only to remember her handbag but to note any landmarks, except for the tiled fountain let into the wall of the *derb*. But there were many such fountains in the medina, just as there were dozens of dark alleys, one looking as much like another as an Arab sheep drover looked like his fellow. To find her way back to the souk from which she had fled was impossible, even if she dared.

However, with her usual optimism, Dizzy took comfort in the fact that both her traveler's checks and her passport were safe in her bedroom bureau drawer. The few dollar bills and loose American change her wallet contained she would not miss sorely—nor would they be of much use to a thief, if theft had been the object of all the unpleasantness.

This attempt to assess her position gave Dizzy a new perspective. Such frantic running was obviously useless; she might be doubling back on her own tracks, which was the last thing she wanted to do. Even without a tip for a helpful child there must be a way to get out of the medina. She would attach herself to an escorted group of tourists, for instance, although that would waste considerable time.

Tourists—but where were they? Dizzy became aware that the streets were far less crowded than in mid-morning, and immediately she realized that noon must have come and gone. The official guides had taken their flocks back to the various hotels for the siesta. She seemed to be the only foreigner abroad.

This, in itself, was upsetting, because being conspicuous might now be actually dangerous. Walking slowly, almost loitering, she came out into the blazing sun from under a bamboo canopy that laced together facing rows of souks. Then, blinking in the glare, she breathed a sigh of intense relief. Straight ahead were high, crenellated walls of reddish-pink muddled clay, beyond which palm plantations and verges of olive trees lifted their leafy heads.

The walls of the city! Seven and a half miles of them, thick and buttressed, but opening through a dozen gates to safety, to the comfortable landmark of the Koutoubia Tower, from which she knew her way back to the house.

But first the police! Dizzy's memory was keen, and she could see in her mind's eye a corner building near the Djemaa-el-Fna from which black-belted, grimly serious officers of the law regularly came and went.

Luck favored her, and high time, too, thought Dizzy. She emerged from the medina very close to the square and hurried to the police station, before which two guards leaned against pillars and a sleepy *calèche* driver dozed.

Then suddenly she was faced by a new problem. What could she say to them? How could she explain? Even in English it would sound absurd to say that she had been drugged in a souk, the location of which she did not know, that her friend had disappeared, and that there were shady doings afoot. Any rational policeman would size her up as a hysterical child.

And in French she would be at an increased disadvantage. Yet it was important to try. Her hair tousled, her face streaked by rivulets of perspiration, her hands empty of the inevitable handbag carried by every tourist, Dizzy approached a uniformed policeman standing with his back to her and casually picking his teeth.

"*Monsieur,*" she began timidly. "*Je suis très distrait, parce que—*"

She got no farther. The man turned slowly and let forth a flood of Arabic, waving his arms and indicating, in quite understandable pantomime, that he didn't understand a word she said.

Dizzy backed away. "*Pardon,*" she managed to tell him. "*Je comprends.*"

This abortive attempt to enlist police help left her only one recourse. She'd have to take the waiting *calèche* and go back to the house for Rick; then together they could go to the Countess, who reputedly spoke some Arabic.

As she swayed along in the back seat of the carriage, directing the driver with hand signals along one street after another, Dizzy was led to hope that this might all be a tempest in a teapot, that after all she might find Felicia at home. The great town, drowsing like an enormous Saharan oasis under the afternoon sun, looked so peaceful and pleasant that she could scarcely believe the events of the past few hours were real.

Yet the acrid taste in her mouth remained, and the backfiring of a *petit taxi* was enough to make her jump. When she dashed into the house to find Rick or Louella—anyone to lend her five dirhams with which to pay her driver!—reason told her that Felicia would not be there.

Nor was she. "Where's Felicia?" asked Louella as she delved into her apron pocket for the purse she always kept there.

"I don't know," Dizzy replied wretchedly, and took the crumpled note out to the gate, thanking the waiting Moroccan in French and indicating that he might keep the change.

Louella, standing in the entrance on Dizzy's return, continued anxiously, "Where's Patrick? I been waiting lunch near an hour now. Where's the car?"

At least Dizzy could answer these last questions. "Rick and the Countess de Redier drove to Amizmiz for a man they need to go along with Dr. Harding's prospecting team. Probably they've been delayed."

"But Felicia? Wasn't she with you, Miss Deborah?"

Dizzy nodded. "We were in the souks, in a big store

where they sell rugs and antique caftans and stuff. I drank some mint tea and then—then I passed out." She didn't want to alarm Louella further by mentioning her conviction that she had been drugged. "When I came to, Felicia had disappeared."

"Disappeared? Well, most likely she went for a doctor," suggested Louella practically. "She probably was scared. You apt to have faintin' spells?"

"No," Dizzy had to admit. "I've never fainted in my life. Oh, Louella, I'd better tell you the rest. I woke up in a little room on a pile of rugs, and there was nobody around, and one of the doors was locked but the other wasn't, and I got out the back way, but I was terribly scared and my purse was gone and I ran and ran. Now I don't think I could even find my way back to the souk because a little boy took us and it was in a part of the medina even Felicia didn't know."

This was too much for Louella to absorb all at once. She drew Dizzy into the coolness of the vaulted hall and sank down on the nearest chair. "Now start over, Miss Deborah, and go slow, please. I got to get this straight."

Dizzy drew a deep breath and began again, but before she had said more than a few words tires crunched on the gravel drive, a car door was slammed, and Rick sauntered into the house.

"Hi," he said casually, mopping his forehead with a damp and rather grubby handkerchief. Then he glanced from Dizzy to Louella, whose expression was grave and worried. "Where's Felicia?" he asked.

Closer to tears than she had been all morning, Dizzy faced one fact squarely. "Oh, Rick," she cried. "Something terrible has happened. Felicia has disappeared."

Six

Rick's reaction to Dizzy's story of the morning's adventure was completely unexpected. He simply refused to take Felicia's disappearance seriously.

Hot, tired, and dusty, he wanted his lunch. "Afterwards, we'll go back to the medina and try to find the place. If I know my sister she's sitting in the front room of that souk reading a book and waiting for you to come to. Or else, as Louella says, she became worried enough to go for a doctor."

Louella found this deduction an immediate comfort. She brought trays of sandwiches and iced tea spiked with mint to the terrace, where Rick ate hungrily, but Dizzy stared miserably at the glasses of tea. Inside she was seething, although she tried to stifle her annoyance at such insensibility. Was this boy stupid or just plain callous? Couldn't he tell that she was genuinely scared? Couldn't he grasp the idea that this was no prank on Felicia's part, that his sister might be in grave danger while he sat here stuffing himself?

"I left one thing out," Dizzy confessed after several minutes. "Because I didn't want to alarm Louella any more than necessary, I didn't mention that I'm sure my tea was drugged."

"What tea? Where?"

"I told you the storekeeper sent the boy who brought us to the shop for some mint tea," Dizzy recapitulated. "It tasted good and I drank mine in a hurry. It was after that I felt faint."

"Look," said Rick wearily, stretching his legs and contemplating his dirty sneakers. "It's a hot day. You're not used to the climate. You were standing around in a heavy jellaba—"

"Caftan."

"Caftan, then. So you passed out. It isn't surprising. The only surprising thing is that you sneaked out of the place and came back here."

"Patrick Harding!" Dizzy was furious, her self-control broken. "I did not sneak. I *escaped*. And I'm not letting my imagination work overtime. The mint tea was drugged. I'm positive!" She got up and stamped her foot. "Oh, you're impossible."

"And you're being childish," Rick retorted, unimpressed by this outburst. "Things like that simply don't happen in Marrakech, can't you understand?"

"Then why was I hidden in a back room. Why?"

"Well, after all, they can't keep a kid who's out cold lying around the shop. It's bad for trade."

Dizzy's eyes narrowed. She could have slapped the

freckled face grinning up at her so impudently. Instead she said icily, "Suppose you explain the locked door."

"Imagination," replied Rick, waving a half-eaten triangle of sandwich in the air. "Pure imagination."

"I'll make you apologize to me for that remark."

"Oh, come now, doll, keep your cool. We'll go find Felicia right now, and then maybe *you'll* be apologizing to *me*."

Driving along the sleeping streets at Rick's side, Dizzy edged over against the door, keeping as much space in the center of the seat as possible. I hate him, I positively hate him, she thought to herself, seething. He's not one bit clever or amusing, he's a bumptious clown, that's what he is, and he thinks I'm making things up out of whole cloth. Well, he'll find out!

Meanwhile, valuable time was being wasted. Rick drove to the Bab Agnou Gate, where he had left the girls that morning, and insisted that Dizzy try to retrace the route they had followed. For about ten minutes, with a combination of luck and her good memory, she managed quite well. Here was the row of spice sellers, here the flashing display of brass and copper. From this next corner five different routes were possible. She and Felicia had taken the one leading past a group of countrywomen squatting on the ground before some garden produce. But where were the women now?

At this point Dizzy became confused. While Rick

trudged along by her side she tried to reconstruct her morning perambulations, but soon she had to admit to herself she was lost.

Before the next intersection she stopped. "It would take a map, a compass, and a Boy Scout to find the way from here."

"Why don't you throw in a Seeing Eye dog?" asked Rick grumpily.

"Do you have one around?" asked Dizzy icily. "As I recall, you said it didn't matter if Felicia and I got lost in the medina. There was always a boy who could show us the way out."

"So what?"

"So we weren't paying attention, that's what."

"Oh, Dizzy, stop being so edgy."

"I'm more than edgy; I'm scared," Dizzy replied with emphasis. "You may think these covered alleys are tunnels of love in an amusement park but I don't, and furthermore—"

Suddenly she broke off and put a hand to her mouth, while her eyes grew round and thoughtful. "The wool souks," she murmured. "Where are the wool souks? Maybe I could find my way from there."

"That's easy." With Dizzy trailing along behind, Rick ducked through a connecting *derb* to another part of the medina, which Dizzy instantly remembered. The magenta skeins still drying in the sun were not mobile, like the farm women. They remained a landmark she could recognize, and unerringly she turned from the wool market along a covered arcade where the over-head wooden doors of cupboardlike pottery shops were propped up on long sticks.

Dodging porters and donkeys, ignoring the impor-tunities of a dozen eager merchants, Dizzy now took the lead. By the moment she became more and more excited, because she knew where she was going at last.

Yes, here was the Berber shop selling *babouches* decorated with beads and gold embroidery. This morn-ing she had paused to examine them closely while Fe-licia called "Come on!" Now Dizzy paused again and waited for Rick to catch up. "It's right around the next corner," she said.

Rick looked relieved, even though he merely grunted, "O.K. Let's go."

But Dizzy drew back, suddenly cautious. Wishing her hair were anything but blond, so she wouldn't be so conspicuous, she glanced around for some kind of disguise. "Lend me your sunglasses, Rick. And buy me one of those big straw hats in that shop across the way, will you? I'll pay you back."

"Oh, for Pete's sake, what are we playing–Mata Hari?"

This was no time for a sharp retort. "Humor me, please!" Dizzy begged with her prettiest smile.

Rick went off muttering "Women!" but at least he went, returning in less than a minute with a hat that was sizes too large but which Dizzy accepted gratefully. When she put it on her companion guffawed. "You look like an elf hiding under a mushroom."

The sunglasses made the effect even more grotesque, because they kept slipping down Dizzy's nose and had to be pushed back up every couple of seconds. Still, she felt much more secure, because she was likely to escape casual detection. Walking slowly, and stopping here and there with the assumed interest of a sightseer, Dizzy led Rick around the corner toward the remembered entryway.

With her heart hammering so loudly she could almost hear it—for what might she expect to find?—and the sunglasses a decided hindrance, Dizzy nevertheless gathered her courage to beard the caftan salesman in his den. "This is it, Rick," she announced in a stage whisper, and there was no uncertainty in her voice.

Then she stopped short in surprise and dismay. Across the entrance was a heavy metal shutter, padlocked to a ring set into a block of concrete on the ground. No hanging lanterns blazed from within; none of the glass display cases were lighted to attract customers. The souk was shut up tight.

"Well, I'll be darned!" Rick sounded puzzled rather than alarmed. "You're *sure*, Dizzy?" He turned and looked at her, although he seemed to anticipate her quick nod.

There was no chance that the shopkeeper had merely

closed up for lunch. This was the sort of place that normally stayed open all day, to attract those "mad dogs and Englishmen" that Felicia was always singing about. Remembering that famous ditty sung in Felicia's familiar voice made Dizzy's heart turn over. "We'd better go straight to the Countess de Redier and get her to contact the police."

Rick hesitated. "I could inquire from the neighbors—"

"No!" Because she was past the point of trusting anyone even vaguely connected with this place, Dizzy was adamant. "You've had your turn, Rick. Now we're going to stop fooling around." Instead of acting like a docile Moroccan possession who considered man the inevitable master, Dizzy intended to take charge from now on.

And to her surprise, Rick didn't object. He seemed nonplussed by the padlocked gate, because he had been confident that his sister could meet with no harm in the souks. "But she wanders all over the medina alone," he kept repeating as Dizzy and he walked swiftly back to the car. "Mother wouldn't let her come here if there were any possibility of danger, don't you see?"

"All I know is what happened," Dizzy replied grimly. "And it wasn't funny. It wasn't funny at all."

Deciding that since it wasn't yet five o'clock, the Countess would still be at his father's office, Rick drove directly to the Avenue Mohammed V, where he pulled up in front of a contemporary building with a bank on the ground floor and suites for businessmen above.

Amarab Petroleum was inscribed in gilt letters on a glass-windowed door on the "*deuxième étage*." Within, a typist was working busily, while the Countess de Redier and Bou Hamida stood talking by the desk in Dr. Harding's private office.

Rick, with scant formality, tossed the typist a "Hi, Lisette," as he hurried past, pushing Dizzy ahead of him.

The Countess and Bou Hamida interrupted their conversation, turning in surprise, but before either of them could greet the newcomers Rick addressed the Frenchwoman directly. "Excuse us, but we've got to speak to you privately."

Bou Hamida bowed. "I was just leaving."

The Countess held out her hand to Dr. Harding's assistant. "Good luck," she said with a smile, "and don't drive too fast."

Rick glanced at the wall clock. "You'll have to fly, not drive, if you expect to make Tinerhir tonight," he suggested.

"Unfortunately," replied Bou Hamida humorlessly, "we have been delayed. Between Ibrahim and several other complications, it will be impossible to go farther than Ouarzazate this evening." Having delivered this statement as though he were a schoolmaster speaking to a pupil, he turned and left.

Rick whistled softly. "Pop'll be fit to be tied," he said in an undertone. Then he kicked the inner door shut. "Dizzy, you'd better tell the Countess your story, and see if it makes any sense to her."

Choosing her words carefully—by now she had practice in telling this tale!—Dizzy described the incident in the souk. Instead of being disbelieving, like Rick, or incredulous, like Louella, the Countess looked distressed. She also, to Dizzy's relief, acted like a competent adult. "Phone the house once more," she ordered Rick, "and make sure Felicia hasn't returned since you left. Tell Louella not to mention this incident to anyone. Then we'll try to get in touch with your father."

Why not mention it, Dizzy wondered, and why not go at once to the police? She asked the latter question while Rick was occupied on the telephone, and the Countess answered it candidly.

"If Felicia has been kidnapped—and that's what it looks like—her captors are hoping we'll raise an alarm at once. They'd like nothing better than a *cause célèbre* to embarrass the King's supporters." She began to pace the floor. "I can see the headlines now. *American Scientist's Daughter Abducted in Marrakech Medina.* How do you think that would sound?"

"Like the truth," said Dizzy, equally candid.

"*Ah, oui.* But the publicity would be terrible for Morocco. It would indicate that the country isn't a safe place for Americans to come."

Well, is it? Dizzy felt like asking, but she held her tongue.

Rick turned from the telephone. "Nope, Odette, no sign of her. Louella says she'll keep her mouth shut. Now what?"

"Now, I'd like to explain to you, as I have to Deborah, that I consider it most unwise to bring the police into this thing, at least at present. In the first place there is a small but rather active group among the Arabs who are definitely pro-Communist and anti-Western. We can't be sure to what degree the local constabulary may be infiltrated with subversive characters. In the second, I don't think Felicia's in any real danger."

The Countess spoke calmly but seriously. Although Dizzy couldn't follow her reasoning, her advice was probably sound. To the police they dared not turn.

"Then we'd better try to contact Pop right away," Rick said. "Can we reach him at Tinerhir, do you think?"

"We can try." The Countess opened the door and gave instructions to the typist in French. Dizzy caught the words Hotel du Sud, *le professeur* and *immédiatement,* but the rest of the conversation was lost on her. However, Lisette picked up the receiver of her desk telephone and the usual 'alloing started, to escape which the Countess came back to Dr. Harding's office and closed the door.

Rick, sitting on the edge of his father's desk, was

pulling a forelock and looking worried, in sharp contrast to his early-afternoon nonchalance. "What about Mother?" he demanded. "She's gone to Paris to be with Aunt Janet, you know. This will be the blow to end all blows."

"I wouldn't get in touch with your mother yet," the Countess said. "Wait until we talk to your father, anyway." She glanced at Dizzy. "Don't assume that I'm taking Felicia's disappearance lightly. It's just that it's difficult to know precisely what to do."

Dizzy nodded. She agreed in principle, yet she yearned for action. To sit in this stuffy office while the minutes dragged by and Lisette made no headway with the long-distance operator seemed more frustrating than anything that had happened all day.

"I wish Bou Hamida were here," the Countess was now saying. "I'd feel much safer with a trustworthy Arab to suggest the best possible move."

It sounded as though Felicia were a pawn in some kind of political chess game played between two adversaries Dizzy couldn't visualize. Cautiously, from under lowered lashes, she reappraised the Countess. Could this Frenchwoman, with her aristocratic bearing and rather hawklike features, be completely reliable? Or was she offering dubious counsel? All her life Dizzy had been taught that the police were the guardians of the law, and to suspect them of treachery within their own ranks was inconceivable.

The Countess opened the office door, and they heard Lisette speaking now in rapid French, holding the mouthpiece at arm's length and shouting at it in the manner customary in this country. She shrugged, gesticulated, and behaved in every way as though she were conducting a conversation with a person in the same room. "*Oui*," Dizzy heard her say. "*Oui, merci beaucoup*." She slammed the receiver into the cradle and pushed back her desk chair.

"*Ce n'est pas possible*." Although Dizzy understood little of the ensuing dialogue, it was obvious that Lisette had been unable to reach Dr. Harding, and that the hotel clerk in Tinerhir had been "*stupide, très stupide*."

"I'll keep trying," the Countess promised Rick and Dizzy. "You go along home now, and don't worry. I'll phone you as soon as I can get through."

"Don't worry," muttered Dizzy as she went down the concrete stairs at Rick's side. "How can she say a thing like that? What are we going to tell Louella? What are we going to *do?*"

Rick shook his head helplessly. "I don't know. It's all so completely incredible. I still can't believe—"

"Oh, for Pete's sake, Rick, stop singing that same song over and over. You'd better face the fact that your sister has been kidnapped. You heard the Countess say it. *Kidnapped*." Dizzy repeated the ugly word for its shock value. Something would have to jolt Rick into revising his mental attitude.

"But how can Odette be sure?"

"She isn't sure. She's making an educated guess." While Rick raced the car home to be within reach of the telephone, Dizzy sat silently beside him with her hands clasped tensely and a frown creasing her forehead. Rick's question had raised doubts in her mind that led her to review the Countess's advice.

Why should Louella be cautioned to keep Felicia's disappearance a secret? Why should Dr. Harding be called instead of the police? Hadn't the word kidnapping come first—and rather too quickly—from the Countess? All this business about political machinations—did it really make sense?

Although she was tempted to confide her doubts to Rick, Dizzy resisted. He was struggling with his own questions, more elementary than hers perhaps, but just as real. And this was a family affair, actually, while she was an outsider—a house guest embroiled in a situation so bizarre that she felt unable to cope with it. Yet who else was there to cope? Certainly neither Rick nor Louella were apt to acquire qualities of instant leadership. The Countess was, from Dizzy's point of view, a question mark. The Hardings must be reached as soon as possible. It was increasingly obvious that telephone contact with Felicia's father had better be established fast.

But the telephones, upstairs and down, were stubbornly silent. Louella had been reduced to wringing her hands and saying, "We got to reach the professor.

What a terrible thing to happen, when he left me in charge of all you three." She sank down in the nearest chair and looked from Rick to Dizzy accusingly, as though they were somehow to blame.

Speaking as calmly as possible, Dizzy said, "This is nobody's fault, Louella. Try not to get too upset. We're bound to get through to Dr. Harding sometime this evening, and he can probably hire a small plane and fly right home."

This last suggestion was a pure fabrication, because Dizzy hadn't the slightest hope that a desert outpost came equipped with an airfield and a row of Piper Cubs awaiting charter. But it seemed to comfort Louella, because she said, "That's just what he's bound to do."

Although she appeared reluctant to leave Rick, who was hovering over the telephone like a bird over a nest, Louella eventually ambled off to finish cooking dinner. Meals, even in times of disaster, had to be served, and although the supper brought to the library on trays was sketchy compared to the Hardings' usual fare, it was appetizing enough to overcome Dizzy's certainty that she couldn't eat a bite.

The twilight hours passed and darkness came, increasing everyone's anxiety. The Countess phoned saying that she was now trying to contact the manager of the Hotel du Sud, who was unavailable until about ten o'clock. The message was relayed to Louella, who was having a cot moved to the hallway outside Dizzy's door.

She intended to spend the night there, like a watch dog. Those Ayrabs might fool a body once but they wouldn't catch her off guard twice in a row.

Having arranged her bedding, she joined Rick and Dizzy in the library, where they were becoming more and more impatient. Ten o'clock passed and the hands of the French clock crawled slowly toward eleven. Dizzy stared blindly at the open pages of a magazine and wondered where Felicia could be. Then she twitched convulsively as the telephone bell jangled once more.

Rick leaped for the instrument. "Yes," he said. "What gives?"

Louella edged forward on her chair, seriously threatening its front legs, and Dizzy closed her magazine softly, while the Countess de Redier's voice rasped over the wires.

"He hasn't reached Tinerhir? How can they be sure?" Rick asked.

Another pause. "Yes. I see. No. I quite agree. We'd better telephone Mother in Paris, right away."

This conclusion made Louella rock back and forth in anguish and mutter, "Oh Lord, oh Lord," under her breath. "Mrs. Harding's gonna have a stroke," she predicted. "It's a fearful thing to have to tell her, over the telephone."

Dizzy agreed, but neither she nor Rick could see any alternative. Dr. Harding had either been held up along the way, or had passed along the Casbah Road through Tinerhir without making his presence known. He seemed to be dashing about southern Morocco unpredictably. Once he had gone beyond reach of a telephone and turned down into the desert, there would be no way of getting a message to him except with camels or jeeps.

"If only I'd had enough sense to alert Bou Hamida!" Rick berated himself. "Say, do you think we could reach him in Ouarzazate. He might be stopping at the hotel where Pop stayed."

It was a good idea, and it lifted Dizzy's hopes—and even Louella's—for a short time. For once the operator made contact speedily, but the desk clerk reported that there was no one registered by the name of Hamida, nor was any such gentleman expected according to his reservation list.

Now Rick accepted the inevitable. "Where's Mother's address in Paris? Didn't she say she'd leave it in the hall?"

"Under the flower bowl on the table. I'll get it," Dizzy said quickly, glad of a chance for action, no matter how slight.

She ran out of the room and across the marble floor to lift the pottery container filled with fragrant June roses. Then she caught her breath and gave a cry of shocked dismay.

There was nothing there.

Seven

"Felicia must have the note with her," Rick said dispiritedly. "You didn't see a piece of paper with Mother's Paris address written on it, did you, Louella?"

"Patrick, you should know better than to ask. Would I be sitting here with my mouth shut if I had?"

Our tempers are getting frayed, Dizzy thought. We're all exhausted. She was, indeed, seeing the room as a blur, but in one active recess of her mind she was trying to recall Felicia's every action before leaving for the souks. She could see her roommate coming down the stairs with a cardigan flung over her shoulders, she could see the large straw bag filled with the usual miscellany, but she couldn't for the life of her see Felicia walking over to the table for the note her mother had promised to leave.

If her memory was correct, what then? Was there someone in the house—someone who wanted to kill any plan to get in touch with Mrs. Harding—who had made off with the slip of paper?

The thought was an uncomfortable one and would not bear uttering aloud, especially at midnight. She was glad when Rick said, "We'd better go to bed, but I'll tell you one thing. If Felicia is still missing in the morning I'm going to start off first thing and drive to Tinerhir. We've got to find Pop."

"I'll go with you," said Dizzy at once, "but remember, your gasoline tank's almost empty. And you'd better check the oil."

Louella rose out of her chair with all the majesty of the sun looming up over the horizon. "You is neither of you getting in that automobile without me," she said. "I am responsible and I will not let you out of my sight again. You hear?"

"Boy, it's going to be quite a party," Rick grumbled, but he knew better than to object. When Louella spoke in that tone of voice, she meant it, and he could no more have moved the Rock of Gibraltar than that mountainous figure.

Practical to the core, Dizzy asked, "Has anybody got any money?"

"I haven't," said Louella promptly. "You borrowed my last five dirhams, Miss Deborah."

Rick jingled a few coins in his pocket ruefully. "I don't even have enough cash to buy gas."

At this point Dizzy took charge. "That means we can't leave until the banks open at nine o'clock, but while I'm getting a check cashed you can have the car serviced, Rick, and Louella can make us a picnic lunch.

How far a drive is it to Tinerhir? Will it take long?"

Rick shrugged. "Six or seven hours."

"Have we got a good map?"

"I'll pick one up at the gas station."

"We'd best pack our nighties," Louella suggested from the doorway. "We'll likely have to stay over."

Dizzy nodded. "A good idea. And now come along, Rick. I won't trust you to drive the High Atlas unless you've had a decent night's sleep."

Rick followed Louella upstairs reluctantly, and Dizzy could tell that he was still hoping for a miracle to occur, for Felicia to appear on the entrance steps, or at least for the telephone to ring. But except for the howling of pariah dogs the silence of the night was unbroken. As she lay hugging her arms between the moonstruck sheets Dizzy was very glad that Louella was sleeping outside her door.

"Miss Deborah!"

Believing that she couldn't have dozed off for a minute, Dizzy nevertheless awakened uncertainly, unsure for the first few seconds where she was. Then she realized it was daylight, that she had somehow managed to greet Louella and prop herself up on the pillows, and that there was a breakfast tray on her knees, just as though this were a normal morning and Felicia also were being awakened across the hall.

"Don't eat too fast, honey, but don't linger," Louella warned her. "It's past seven o'clock."

Dizzy buttered a croissant and sipped her *café au lait* (except for Dr. Harding's hearty morning meal breakfasts in this house were continental) but she wasn't really hungry. She put the tray aside for Ali to pick up later, showered quickly, and put on a washable dress. Packing took only a few minutes—her dressing case, a white sweater, pajamas, robe and slippers. By seven forty-five she was pacing up and down the terrace waiting for Rick to appear.

And in the clear light of morning she was thinking, thinking and changing her mind about the projected expedition. No matter what the Countess advised, before chasing off across the mountains in search of Mr. Harding, she intended to notify the police.

Because how could Rick know, beyond a shadow of a doubt, that the Countess was really loyal to her employer? Suppose the opposite were true? Suppose the Frenchwoman was in on some sort of plot which involved the kidnapping of Felicia? Then naturally she'd want to avoid any contact with the law.

The moment she saw Rick, sleepy eyed and frowning, Dizzy ignored his appearance of distress and plunged at once into the proposition that before going to the bank they must go to the nearest police station and appeal for help.

"But Odette was so sure—"

"I don't care," Dizzy interrupted. "I'm not going to leave Marrakech without trying. Both of your parents would think we were behaving like a pair of hysterical children. What are the police for, anyway, if not to solve crimes and apprehend criminals?"

Rick yawned, appearing too exhausted to argue. "O.K.," he agreed, "but we'd better get going. This sort of thing takes time."

Half an hour later, cooling her heels in a dusty anteroom while Rick stared gloomily from a barred window, Dizzy watched the hands of a wall clock move jerkily past eight thirty. The only officer who spoke French had not yet come in, but she gathered he was due any minute, and each new arrival set her heart hammering against her chest.

"I'm prepared to wait until nine o'clock," Rick said, "but not a second longer. This is nothing but a colossal waste of time."

Dizzy didn't answer. Although inclined to agree, she was also convinced that they were pursuing the only mature and reasonable course. As a thin, jaunty officer with freshly polished boots stepped smartly across the hall and disappeared behind a closed door her spirits lifted. "I'll bet that's him."

She was right. Minutes later Dizzy and Rick stood in his presence before a cluttered desk and tried to explain their errand in school-book French. The man listened courteously for a time, stifling an obvious inclination to smile, then appraised Dizzy somewhat rudely, looking her over from the top of her curly head to the sandals on her bare feet.

Rick was becoming increasingly impatient. His eyes were narrowed, and he now looked thoroughly awake. "It's my sister," he repeated. "We believe she has been kidnapped. You understand? Kidnapped."

The policeman shrugged. "It is not possible," he insisted. "Not in Marrakech. Marrakech is a very safe city, with many tourists." A happy idea occurred to him. "She has perhaps run away!"

Dizzy shook her head vigorously, and haltingly tried to describe the incident in the souk. But the French was beyond her. She kept injecting English words that meant nothing to the officer. When she broke off, spreading her hands in dismay, he smiled, looked straight into her eyes, and unmistakably winked.

"That ties it." Rick grabbed Dizzy's arm. "Let's get out of here and go find Pop!" Pulling her behind him he strode angrily through the door and across the lobby. "Well, I hope you're satisfied," he muttered as they reached the car.

Dizzy bit her lip. "But they're so stupid!" she raged. "At home–"

"You're not at home. You're in North Africa," Rick reminded her. "And at home one of our policemen wouldn't make much sense out of a girl in a jellaba and nose veil spouting Arabic."

Dizzy was pondering this remark as they pulled up outside the bank, a modern building fronted by an arcade, just as the doors were opening. "Hurry back," she entreated as she slammed the car door. "This won't take a minute." Already she had her folder of traveler's checks in her hand.

"Famous last words," Rick muttered ruefully, and gunned the motor as he drove away.

A few clients, waiting on the sidewalk, entered the bank along with Dizzy, and went with their business to various stations along a twenty-foot counter, lacking the tellers' booths Dizzy was accustomed to at home. She approached a likely looking Moroccan, said, "*S'il vous plait*," then instead of struggling with the French language displayed her book of checks.

The clerk nodded understandingly and directed her to the end of the room, turning her over to another employee already busy with a client who had gone straight to the proper location. Engaged in some business nearby was a tall, immaculate Arab gentleman wearing a white turban and a summer-weight gray jellaba. As Dizzy waited she looked at him carefully and realized that the profile was familiar.

Then, while some papers were being processed, he turned, recognized her, and bowed. It was Dr. Mohammed el Hazziz, the King's representative, who had been the Hardings' dinner guest three nights before. How long ago that seemed! Dizzy held out her hand. "*Bon jour*, Dr. Hazziz," she said, relieved that she remembered his name. "I thought you lived in Rabat, not Marrakech."

The diplomat nodded. "That is correct," he said in

English, "but I come here frequently on state business. Marrakech is, so to speak, our southern capital."

"Oh, I see," replied Dizzy lamely. She really hadn't anything further to say.

"Professor Harding has left for the South?" Dr. Hazziz asked her after a moment.

Dizzy nodded. "Two days ago."

"And your charming young schoolmate—where is she?"

For a split second Dizzy hesitated, tempted to confide the story of Felicia's disappearance, but discretion held her back. Seeds of distrust, although recently planted, were flourishing in her brain. Why did Dr. Hazziz inquire for Felicia rather than Mrs. Harding? Could anyone be trusted in such a mysterious country? Was this Moroccan, after all, exactly what he seemed? Replying, she said, "Felicia didn't come with me this morning," and turned to the clerk, who was finally ready to attend to her needs.

"Fifty dollars' worth of dirhams, please," said Dizzy as she signed a traveler's check.

The clerk nodded, scrutinized the check, asked in French for her passport, then began filling out an imposing series of forms in quadruplicate, using violet ink. This was a lengthy process, but eventually he handed her two of the forms along with a small token like a numbered hat check. Gesturing toward a window on the far side of the bank, he muttered something.

Dizzy, feeling sure Rick must already be waiting outside, hurried across to present her token, only to be waved away. Then she noticed that half a dozen people were sitting or standing around dejectedly, while the clerk she had approached disappeared.

At long last he emerged from a back office, sorted through some papers he was carrying, and bawled a number in French. A somnolent Arab jumped up as though he had been bitten, presented his token ceremoniously, and stood silent while a few dirhams were slowly and carefully counted into his hand.

This process was repeated for several other customers while Dizzy paced back and forth, glancing again and again at the hands of a clock set into the rear wall. Time raced while the banking ceremonies dragged. By now Rick would be seething with anxiety to be off. He might even come storming in to see if she too had been spirited away.

"*Cinquante six.*"

Although his Arabic accent was hard for her American ears to follow, Dizzy assumed that at last she was being called. Presenting her hat check hopefully, she waited while the teller leafed through a sheaf of forms on the shelf beside him, shook his head, and once more motioned her away.

"But why—? I'm in a terrible hurry! Can't you—" She broke off, realizing that she was speaking a foreign language the clerk couldn't possibly understand. Two more customers had their needs attended to, each operation requiring several minutes, then finally Dizzy was called to the window again.

Very methodically the teller checked her claim check with several documents, compared the photo in her passport with the girl whose head and shoulders appeared above the counter, then elaborately counted out 259 dirhams, a pile of paper money topped with a few coins.

"*Merci*," Dizzy said shortly, and stuffed the money into her handbag without recounting it, which seemed to disturb the clerk unreasonably. As she turned to hurry out of the bank he stood looking after her as though she were a shady operator who should not be trusted with his bank's money—no indeed!

Rick was sitting hunched over the wheel of the car. "Where under the sun have you been?"

"Waiting while they printed up some extra dirhams," retorted Dizzy. "Of all the silly ways of running a business! They do enough paper work in there to plug up Boulder Dam. Oh well, at least we've got some cash."

Rick had to pay off the gas-station operator, an acquaintance of his who had extended him temporary credit. Then he headed for home.

Belatedly, at precisely ten thirty, they started off, Louella ensconced like a queen in the rear seat and their light luggage stowed in the trunk. The mercury had already climbed to 100 degrees in the shade.

Yet it was a dry heat, and Dizzy was growing accustomed to it. Louella, having grown up in the South, didn't complain, and Rick was so absorbed in his driving and in his anxiety to reach his father that he ignored the weather. Besides, the mountains were up ahead.

Straight and bright as a metal tape measure the road led toward them, as they suddenly loomed out of the haze like a gigantic backdrop for a drama. Rows of eucalyptus trees gave way to stony desert, dotted with flocks of goats and sheep foraging for every visible scrap of green.

The ragged shepherds herding these animals, small boys with staves to beat their charges back from the road, waved vigorously as they spotted Dizzy's blond hair. "*Argent, argent,*" they cried if they were within calling distance, but Dizzy waved back and shook her head. They had no time to stop.

Occasional mud houses were surrounded by hedges of thistles or prickly pear. Near each of them, Rick explained, there must be a well or a spring. An occasional casuarina tree also testified to the presence of water, and in the shade of one of these a ring of camels stood, munching on the lower branches as though they found the dusty leaves succulent. Otherwise the terrain was arid, stretching on either side as far as the eye could reach. The prospect made Dizzy shudder. How could people growing up in such an uncompromising landscape be anything but fierce? Concern for Felicia engulfed her afresh, but to discuss the kidnapping further was like twirling a whip in a circle. It led nowhere, but it hurt.

Rick apparently had come to the same conclusion, and Louella, who had been up since dawn, was comatose in the back seat. She roused slightly when the car started to weave through the foothills of the High Atlas, then closed her eyes either in resignation or in prayer.

Deliberately, to keep herself from thinking, Dizzy tried to enjoy the changing scenery. Pink oleanders, some still in bloom after their lavish March flowering, grew in the clefts of rocks. Slim black cedars rose against the harsh blue sky. A lumbering bus, the rack on its top piled high with bicycles and bundles, Arabs spilling from every open window, edged past while Rick clung to an outside curve. "Don't they approve of guard rails over here?" Dizzy asked.

"If they do, they keep it a secret," Rick replied. He was being especially cautious, tooting his horn at every blind turn, but the road was becoming more precipitous by the minute and occasional fallen rocks looked as though they had been scattered deliberately.

Noon approached and the country became wilder, the road steeper and more winding. Louella shifted her bulk with a profound sigh and opened her eyes. "Looks like parts of West Virginia," she remarked.

To Dizzy this seemed far-fetched. Certainly nowhere

in West Virginia would one see a veiled woman squatting beside a red-wrapped bundle that looked like a huge tomato. Nowhere would a white-thatched, bearded wayfarer have on his head a crocheted *tagia.* Nowhere would ancient women, wearing leggings to guard them against snakebite, be staggering along a main road under burdens that bent them double—human burros carrying home the wood for next winter's fires.

"You-all getting hungry?" asked Louella.

"Let's wait awhile," Rick proposed. "We've only been traveling two hours. I'd like to get the Tizi N'Tichka Pass behind us before we stop."

The road continued to climb, doubling in hairpin bends up the craggy face of the mountain. Far below was a swift river bordered with Alep pines, green oaks, and an occasional brush stroke of pink oleander. Unexpectedly a village came into sight, one street of facing houses lying straight along a ridge. "This is Taddert," Rick said. "I've been this far before."

Some young boys along the road were holding out handfuls of glittering stones. "What are they?" Dizzy asked.

"Amethysts," Rick replied. "Just the crude stuff as it comes out of the mines. We'll be coming into manganese country pretty soon."

At another time Dizzy would have begged to stop and examine the stones more closely, but today Felicia's plight drove any such thought from her mind. Speed in reaching Dr. Harding was imperative, and on this twisting, turning grade Rick seldom dared to drive faster than thirty miles an hour.

The river disappeared and the gray mountains rose treeless to the pass, nearly 7,000 feet above the plain. Now they were on the crest of the range. Spread like a crazy quilt below was a panorama of ridges and valleys that led to the deep South. Noble, timeless, serene, the view made Dizzy forget everything else for a space of minutes. "Isn't it beautiful!" she murmured. "Isn't it perfectly magnificent."

Louella craned forward from the back seat to have a look, but heights made her dizzy, and she sank back again after an appreciative murmur. She's being a very good sport, Dizzy thought, and turned to smile at her encouragingly. "From now on it should be all downhill."

"Downhill but on the outside," Rick muttered, as he braked and honked for still another unguarded turn. "O.K., let's eat," he suggested a few minutes later, and pulled into a dirt track leading off to the left, where a grassy border offered a safe place to park.

"Telouet," read a decrepit road sign, "16 k."

There was no sign of a tree, but the air at this height was cooler than on the plain, so everyone got out of the car to stretch. Louella unpacked the lunch on a convenient rock, but insisted that Dizzy and Rick eat standing up. "I hear the professor tell about snakes in the mountains," she said, looking around warily. "There's no use taking any chances. We got enough trouble as it is."

Dizzy was inclined to agree. The Atlas had cut them off from the last vestige of civilization as she knew it—from airports and railroads and the cities of the North. "What is Telouet?" she asked. "A village or a town?"

"Neither," Rick said between bites of a chicken sandwich. "It's a big casbah—a fortified castle—built by the Glaouis, a famous ruling family of Morocco. It was started about a hundred years ago when they were still in power, then abandoned before it was half finished. I'd like to go there sometime. It's said to have 600 rooms."

"Lordy, imagine keeping all them clean," sighed Louella. "What would people want such a big place for?"

"Can't you guess?" asked Rick, to tease her. "El Glaoui had a harem—maybe a hundred wives."

"You go on now."

"Want to bet?"

Louella snorted. "I don't hold with such heathen conduct, and you know it, Patrick. You just stop such tomfool talk in front of a young lady like Miss Deborah here."

Dizzy tried to stifle her laughter but it was impossible. "I'm not shocked, Louella. Besides, I'm sure Rick's exaggerating."

Only slightly mollified, Louella began to pack up the remains of the lunch. Dizzy could tell that she was preparing for the contingency that they would find nothing whatever to eat on the other side of these green mineral hills.

Once his passengers were seated, Rick swung the car around carelessly, anticipating no traffic, but suddenly a cry of "*Balek!*" smote the air. Entering the side road from the main highway was the inevitable Arab mounted on a donkey, who seemed to appear even in the most remote spots as though manufactured out of thin air.

Rick put on his brakes and waited for the fellow to pass. Aside from that one importunate cry he neither spoke nor signaled, but just sat staring into the distance dourly, while his heels beat a soundless tattoo on the donkey's flank. Dizzy stared after the old man and said, bemused, "I keep seeing that same Arab everywhere."

"Him or his brother," Rick returned. "After a certain age they all look alike."

Eight

Dizzy dozed, awakened, then dozed again, while the sun beat through the windshield and the dusty air parched her throat. They had come down to a plain once more—the *bled es siba*, as the lawless country of unsubdued tribes was traditionally called. A land of red earth sprinkled with spiky argan trees stretched on either side, and the road straightened out and became flat as it approached Ouarzazate.

"How about driving for a while, Diz?" Rick proposed. "This is as good a place as any to get the feel of the car."

Unaccustomed to a stick shift, Dizzy hesitated, but she knew Rick must be tired, and he was right in saying that the road offered no problems. They hadn't seen another vehicle for the past twenty miles.

Once behind the wheel, Dizzy's self-confidence returned. She wished her mother could see her handling this little Fiat. Then maybe she wouldn't be so loath to let her borrow the family station wagon when she was home from school.

To be getting any pleasure at all out of this errand into the deep South seemed disloyal to Felicia. Dizzy felt that all their thoughts should be with her roommate, and all their efforts bent on pushing ahead.

Yet it was with reluctance that she drove past the first great casbah they had seen. Perched high on a rock at the end of a side road leading off the main highway was a castle with battlements that might have been constructed in Hollywood.

"Oh, look!" Dizzy cried. "Can that be real?"

"Hey, watch out!" Rick cautioned as the car swerved noticeably toward the edge of the road. Then he consulted the guidebook he kept in the glove compartment. "That must be Tifoultout," he decided. "It says here it's an authentic nobleman's residence—another one of the casbahs built by the Glaoui of Marrakech. Boy, they were busy kids! Peter O'Toole and the technicians were put up here when they filmed some of the desert sequences for *Lawrence of Arabia*. Imagine that."

Dizzy could easily imagine it. From a distance the casbah looked infinitely intriguing and glamorous. "Is it open to the public, do you think?"

Rick continued to leaf through the guidebook. "Yes. Apparently it's now the annex of the Hotel du Sud in Ouarzazate. But if you think we've got time to go take a look at it, you're wrong."

"That's unfair, Rick," Dizzy retorted. "I'm just as anxious as you are to reach your father." She took one last glance at the crenellated battlements, then addressed her attention sternly to the road, along which scattered mud houses began to appear, and the ubiquitous herds of goats and sheep gave way to the donkey traffic that indicated a caravansary of some sort ahead.

Ouarzazate was, comparatively speaking, a big town, with a wide main street lined with stores, a hotel set high on a hill, and a row of suburban villas, probably owned by French people who had come here during the days when Morocco was a protectorate.

Rick suggested that Dizzy pull into a gas station to refuel. As soon as she had turned off the ignition he got out of the car and tried to communicate with the young man who was using a hand pump to fill the tank. Since the lad understood neither French nor English, and Rick's command of Arabic consisted of isolated words, the interchange was conducted primarily in sign language.

"Land Rover with American–zoom?" Cutting the palms of his hands along each other to indicate speed, Rick watched the young man's eyes hopefully, but puzzlement was the only expression readable.

"*Vous connais* Land Rover?"

"Lan Wover," attempted the Arab, nodding.

"Land Rover zoom Ouarzazate?"

The boy shook his head. Either he didn't understand or he had seen no such car.

Rick tried again. "Chevrolet? No American. Arabs." He held up three fingers.

The young man shrugged. "*Inch' Allah.*"

"What does he mean by that?" Dizzy asked, leaning out from the driver's seat.

"Darned if I know." Rick looked around. "Your boss-man, he speak English, French?"

The boy continued pumping gas steadily, but shook his head.

"Look," said Rick. "Chevrolet sleep here?" He cradled his head on his folded hands and closed his eyes.

This made the Arab burst out laughing. "Fiat slip hotel," he said.

"Oh, no," Rick retorted. "Fiat go Tinerhir. To-night." He made the cutting motion with his hands once more. "Zoom."

"No zoom," said the attendant. "*Route en réparation.*" He wiggled a forefinger descriptively in the air, then hung the gasoline hose in its cradle. From the back seat Louella asked Dizzy, "How far is Tinerhir from where we are now?"

"I'm not quite sure." Dizzy picked up the crumpled road map on the seat beside her and tried to estimate. "Maybe four hours."

"But that doesn't allow for detours," said Rick, overhearing. "Say, do you suppose the road could be so bad that Pop was held up a full day?"

This was an unanswerable question, but it gave everyone pause. By the time the water and oil were checked and the gas was paid for, the hands of Dizzy's watch were creeping toward five.

"We could try phoning the Tinerhir hotel again," Rick proposed. "If Pop should be there now we'd save a lot of time, because he could start right back."

Dizzy and Louella both agreed, but to put through a call on a pay telephone in the town was beyond Rick's capabilities. He couldn't explain his needs in sign language to an operator on the other end of the wire. No alternative was left but to climb the hill to the hotel, a pink plaster structure before which a big bus labeled *Maroc Tours* was disgorging an inordinate number of passengers.

While Dizzy and Louella asked to be directed to the ladies' room, Rick waited in line to speak to the French desk clerk and ask him to put through the call. He made the request very politely, but the Frenchman looked scandalized.

"*Ce n'est pas possible!*" he cried. "*Le Groupe est arrivé et je suis très occupé. Attendez là jusqu'a ce que je vous appelle.*"

Impatient as he was to be off, Rick had no recourse. Dizzy and Louella joined him at a table in the rear of the crowded lobby and put in the time by sipping *citron pressés*, while Rick ordered a coke.

At last the final member of *Le Groupe* was assigned a room and led off by a porter, so Rick once more approached the desk. By now the harassed clerk was in dignant at any further demands on his time, especially when made by a young American who was not even a guest at the hotel. But although his manner was surly, he picked up the telephone and managed, within five minutes, to reach Tinerhir. Then he handed the instrument to Rick, who asked in schoolboy French whether Monsieur Docteur Harding had yet arrived.

From Rick's changing expression Dizzy could tell that the answer was negative. "*Oui, merci,*" she heard him say. "*Je regrette—*" Then he frowned and hung up. "Boy," he said as he returned to Dizzy and Louella, "they sure don't like us to keep on calling. I have a feeling if Pop did turn up now they'd shoot him on sight."

Dizzy considered this no time to mention possible violence, even in fun. Nearly an hour had been wasted. "What about rooms for the three of us in Tinerhir? Did you forget to ask?"

Rick groaned. "I'm a dope," he admitted. Sheepishly he walked back to the desk, while Dizzy and Louella waited even more restlessly.

After a long consultation that Dizzy tried vainly to overhear, Rick returned to the table looking uncertain. "He says there'll be no trouble about rooms, but that we can't possibly make it before dark."

Louella, who had gathered up her handbag, put it back on the table firmly. "That settles it," she said. "We ain't budging. I am responsible for you two and I refuse."

"Oh, now come, Louella. Be a sport." Rick's tone was wheedling.

"No sirree," replied Louella adamantly. "I like the Ayrabs fine, but only in the daylight. Or inside a house. Not on the open road at night."

Rick spread his hands helplessly. "This hotel is full up. They'd have to send us out to the annex." Then he said to Dizzy, "But I suppose you'd go for that."

"You mean—you mean the Casbah of Tifoultout?" Dizzy's eyes began to shine, but she didn't want to seem too eager so she lowered her lashes decorously. "If we really *have* to stay over—if it's *impossible* to reach Tinerhir tonight, I mean—then I think it would be marvelous."

Louella looked less enthralled. "What about snakes?" she asked. "Ali says those old casbahs are full of them."

Losing patience, Rick said, "Look, Louella, you can't have it both ways. Either we push on to Tinerhir and arrive sometime late tonight or we take our chances on snakes and bats and things that go boom in the night. These are the only rooms available."

"Pay no attention to him," Dizzy advised, patting Louella's plump arm. "There aren't going to be any snakes in a hotel."

But had she seen their accommodations first she could not have been so comforting. Magnificent from a distance, the casbah proved to be crumbling under the hot Moroccan sun. The mud-brick walls were pockmarked with ugly holes, and the once palatial interior had been stripped of its noble furnishings. Yet the plan was handsome. The residence was built around a big square patio with a tiled floor and a fountain, above which a four-sided gallery opened into rooms converted from those once used for a rich man's harem. These still kept their authentic Oriental decor, even though the painted plaster was peeling from the walls, the tiles were cracked or broken, and the original lanterns were replaced by unshaded electric light bulbs hanging from strands of frayed wire. Each small chamber came equipped with a sink, the taps dripping rusty water, but bathroom facilities were shared with all other guests on the floor. In the room to which Dizzy was assigned, a cot with sagging springs was made up with coarse white sheets. There was no closet, only a couple of wire coat hangers casually swinging from a wall hook.

However, Dizzy would not allow herself to complain, even privately. To spend the night in an authentic casbah seemed incredibly romantic, although she did hope Peter O'Toole hadn't been forced to make do with a cot as short as hers. While Louella collapsed and took a nap she went up to the battlements, where after a while Rick joined her. Together they leaned on the parapet and watched the sun sink in the west.

Completely enthralled, Dizzy was unaware that Rick was watching her rather than the sunset. Then he said, unexpectedly, "This light on your hair makes you look as if you're wearing a halo. I bet you made a slick angel in Christmas pageants when you were a little girl."

Dizzy laughed. "I was terribly miscast," she admitted. "I'm not the angelic type. And I've always hated my hair because it's entirely too curly. I wish it were long and straight and silky like Felicia's."

"Nonsense," Rick said gruffly. "You look great, just the way you are. Stop fishing for compliments."

Now why did he have to say that and spoil it all, Dizzy wondered. Actually, she had been flattered by Rick's first remark, because it meant that he had begun to look at her as a girl, not just as his sister's roommate to whom he was in duty bound to be polite. For her part, she was finding Rick's constant companionship less trying than she had feared. He drove intelligently, he took charge when necessary, and in general acted more like a man than a boy. Glancing up at him, Dizzy found herself touched by reluctant admiration. What difference did his teasing make when by and large he was behaving so well?

Embarrassment made Rick suddenly awkward. He indicated the heavens with a sweeping gesture and changed the subject. "Pretty dramatic show."

The spectacle was breathtaking because the sky was so vast. Stained with crimson and orange, the dome above their heads changed with every passing minute. A fiery ball, the sun seemed to be pulled down behind the mountains by invisible cords, moving faster and faster until nothing remained but an astonishing streak of green light, glimpsed for a split second and then gone.

At once the air became cool, and Dizzy shivered as much from excitement as from chill. "Let's go inside and rescue Louella," she suggested. "How soon do you suppose we can eat? I'm starved."

She was even hungrier by the time the dining room opened at eight o'clock. Here the floor was strewn with bright, deep-piled rugs and the guests were seated along the walls on low divans covered with worn crushed velvet. In order to be installed on one of these couches Louella required the help of Rick and a waiter, but once settled she seemed comparatively cheerful and ready to accept whatever fate had in store.

The cooking was Moroccan, as was the service, another plus so far as Dizzy was concerned. First they were brought the usual pitcher of rose water, copper basin, towel and soap. "I already washed my hands," Louella complained.

But Rick whispered, "Well, now you're washing your knife and fork."

After this formality a cloth was laid on the tray table pulled up in front of them and a piece of crusty bread was put at each place. "This is called *kesrah*," Rick explained. "You can sop up the sauce with it if you like."

Somewhat later the main dish arrived on a big round plate of varnished terra cotta covered with a conical wicker lid.

"It looks like a Chinese hat," Dizzy murmured, then

sniffed an interesting aroma. The waiter whisked the cover away and in front of them was a whole chicken cooked with lemon and olives and swimming in a thin yellow sauce.

"It smells good but how do we eat it?" Dizzy asked.

"With your fingers," Rick replied. "But only the first three fingers of the right hand if you want to be correct."

"*Bismi Allah*," said Louella unexpectedly, and both of the young people turned to her. "What does that mean?" they asked simultaneously.

"It's the way Ali says 'God bless,'" responded Louella. "All Ayrabs say grace before they eat, and since we're here we may as well do things their way."

"Do you know any other Arab words?" Dizzy asked curiously as she watched Rick pull off a chicken leg.

"A few, a few," said Louella. "After all, I've been in Marrakech 'most a year."

"Can you understand the language at all?" Dizzy persisted.

"Only sometimes. When Ali talks slow-like I get a few words now and then." Louella reached for the second leg as the part of the bird easiest to manage, while Dizzy bravely tore off a strip of the succulent breast. It seemed positively wicked to be enjoying this food while Felicia's fate was still unknown, but Dizzy couldn't help herself.

Meanwhile, sounds of unusual outside activity came drifting through the open doors. A tall thin man with a spanking white turban and jellaba setting off his blue-black skin crossed the courtyard, consulted with one of the waiters, and returned the way he had come. Through slits in the thick wall, which served as ground-floor windows, came a sound like birds twittering. Listening more closely, Dizzy recognized female voices, subdued but laughing. "I wonder what's happening?"

Rick said, "Haven't a clue. Shall I go have a look?"

"Better wait until we've finished," Dizzy suggested. The chicken bones were now being taken away and another dish put down in their place. The meal ended with fruit, and by the time mint tea was served the activity outside had increased. Even Louella became impatient to find out what was going on, and when it finally became time to leave she waddled ahead of Rick and Dizzy curiously.

Now the inner court was lit by swinging lanterns and the fountain was stilled. Benches were ranged under the gallery on all four sides, which made Rick suggest, "Maybe there's going to be some dancing. That's something worth seeing, Diz."

Dizzy nodded. Looking through the arched entrance into the courtyard, she motioned to her companions to follow her outside. Here, under the light of a high-riding moon, nearly fifty women dressed in Moroccan finery—embroidered caftans and *monsourrias*, heavy Berber bracelets and necklaces—were squatting along one wall and talking cheerfully among themselves.

In two arched recesses in the battlements wood fires

had been lighted. Their flames leaped high into the still air as turbaned figures moved around them, heating and testing the goatskin that covered crude drums. All were men, unusually tall and very black. Like the women they seemed merry and vivacious, smiling and calling back and forth to one another as though they were having great fun.

"They must be entertainers," Rick said. "If so we're really in luck. They dance the *ahouach* sometimes in the casbahs of the High Atlas, but then why isn't there an audience?"

His question was answered as if on cue by the arrival of the *Tour Maroc* bus, disgorging its passengers in a ragged stream that led straight to the inner court. There were Germans and Scandinavians, English, and a few French. "Excuse me. Is there going to be dancing?" Dizzy asked a bald-headed Briton with a moustache.

"Mm. Yes, m'dear. So I understand." He glanced at the mountain women, who were now getting to their feet and arranging their costumes. "Very interesting, what?"

"Yes, indeed!" Dizzy nodded, while she drew Rick and Louella into the entering throng. "Let's get a place to sit down while we still can."

They found seats on a bench at the far side, while the women dancers arranged themselves in a shoulder-to-shoulder circle around the smaller group of men carrying tambourines and *bendirs*. For a moment an intense quiet fell; then the tallest man gave a sudden call as though he were invoking some divinity. At once the musicians began to play, and the swaying women took up the opening theme in a rhapsodic chorus. As they sang they began to tap their bare feet on the tiled floor; then the entire circle moved with stately grace in a counter-clockwise shuffle around the room. The men limited themselves to accompanying the dancers with a rhythm that gradually became more intense, and the casbah walls resounded to a chanting that grew shriller by the moment.

Dizzy was thrilled, but Louella became positively ecstatic. She closed her eyes and rocked back and forth as though she found the cadence irresistible.

To Dizzy the music seemed strange and rather dissonant, but along with the rest of the audience she was captivated by the pace of the dance. Still keeping their shoulders touching, the women were clapping their hands now, and their feet moved more and more nimbly as the musicians increased the beat.

Then suddenly and unexpectedly the dance was over, as though everyone had stopped in mid note. During the subsequent applause the women smoothed their dresses and rearranged their headgear and the men stood about grinning and talking in a tight-knit group.

Dizzy let her eyes stray about the court, trying to assess the impression being made on this oddly assorted collection of middle-aged vacationists, the men in slacks and sports jackets, the women in typical tourist dresses, their hands grasping oversized traveling handbags protectively.

In the courtyard doorway a group of Arabs were standing, and as Dizzy glanced their way one of them extricated himself from the throng and walked into the light, smiling. Dizzy gasped and clutched Rick's arm.

"Look!" she cried. "Over there! There's Bou Hamida!"

Nine

Amazement brought Rick to his feet and made him stumble over the outstretched legs of a tourist and brush past the line of dancers unceremoniously. "Bou Hamida!" he cried. "What are you doing here?"

Dizzy, trailing along behind, saw the smile leave Bou Hamida's face and equal astonishment fill his eyes. "Patrick! What are *you* doing here?" he echoed, and the two young men grasped hands eagerly as the circle of dancers started to re-form.

"Here! Come on outside where we can talk." Rick drew his father's assistant through the close-packed throng in the entrance, and Dizzy followed on their heels, murmuring, "Excuse me, please," as she edged her way along.

"My answer's easy," Bou Hamida said as the three gained the comparative quiet of the courtyard. "The Chevy has a broken axle, and we're held up in Ouarzazate until they can get one down to us by the morning bus from Marrakech. But you—?" He turned to Dizzy and bowed in greeting. "Pardon, mademoiselle, but I was so startled at seeing Patrick that my manners have deserted me. Where is Felicia, or," he asked with a heavy-handed attempt at humor, "have you two eloped?"

"Felicia has disappeared," Dizzy told him at once, and Bou Hamida's expression immediately became grave. "Disappeared? What do you mean?"

Between them Rick and Dizzy spilled out the whole incredible story, from the episode in the souk to the Countess de Redier's disinclination to notify the police.

Bou Hamida listened carefully, although he seemed increasingly astounded. "I think the Countess was very wise. There could be political overtones if it became generally known that Professor Harding's daughter has been kidnapped—overtones that might hurt the oil project immeasurably."

Everybody seems to be more concerned about the discovery of oil than they do about Felicia, Dizzy thought to herself. She'd wager Dr. Harding wouldn't look at it that way. He'd head for home and get help from the King before you could say scat.

"I realize you can't reach your father by phone," Bou Hamida was saying to Rick. "I've tried to inform him about our delay, to no avail. But what I can't understand is why you're here in Tifoultout at this—this party. I should think you would have driven straight through to Tinerhir."

"We didn't get started until late this morning," Rick explained. "Gas and money and things held us up. Then we found out the road from here on is supposed to be pretty bad in spots, and Louella couldn't be persuaded to travel after dark."

"Louella? You mean the cook is here with you *too?*" Bou Hamida seemed to be staggered by this information.

"She's acting as chaperone," Dizzy told him. "After what happened to Felicia she's scared to let us out of her sight."

"Then where is she now?"

"Inside, watching the dancing. You'd better come speak to her, Bou Hamida. She'll be awfully relieved to have a responsible adult on hand."

"One moment." Bou Hamida appeared to be thinking. "If it weren't for that axle I'd push on tonight. Once your father gets into the desert he'll be out of touch, and it's vital to reach him. He's the only person who can decide what to do."

"I know," said Rick wretchedly. "We're not here from choice, you understand. And we plan to leave for Tinerhir at dawn."

Dawn! Dizzy stifled a compulsive yawn. From within the casbah the beat of drums and the high-pitched wailing of the women had started again, sending a thrill down her spine. Until the music stopped, sleep would be impossible. Only a totally deaf person could doze off in that din.

Bou Hamida moved into the light of a wall lantern and wrote something on a card, meanwhile saying seriously to Rick, "The minute you get into town go to this address. A cousin of mine was to find a jeep we could hire to team up with the Land Rover, and he'll no doubt know where your father has gone. If he's waiting for the rest of us at the last oasis, leave the women at the hotel in Tinerhir and get down there as fast as you can. The *piste* is a rough, dirt track, as you know, but if you're not overloaded you can manage. I suppose you're driving the Fiat?"

Rick nodded, and Dizzy could tell he was relieved to have some experienced advice. He took the card, tucked it away safely in his wallet, and asked, "How long will it take to get the new axle installed? It would be good if you could reach Tinerhir before we start back."

Bou Hamida shrugged. "You know these small town garages. There's no telling, really. If we don't meet in Tinerhir or on the road you can find me at the Greek's—that's the old hotel on the main street—or at the service station only a couple of hundred yards from there."

"Right," Rick said. "Now come on in and see Louella. We jumped up and ran off without saying a word to her. She probably thinks we've deserted to the East."

Bou Hamida joined the pair as they started back inside, but he had lost the smiling demeanor worn when he had first arrived. Felicia's disappearance has upset him quite as much as it has us, Dizzy thought. He looks worried sick.

To escape the noise the three had moved over to a lantern hung on the outer wall, and now, as they started back across the courtyard, the effect of the casbah turrets rising into the moonlit sky made Dizzy catch her breath.

"Isn't it beautiful?" she cried, turning to Bou Hamida. "Isn't it the most beautiful casbah you've ever seen?"

"It's very striking tonight," he said, "but Tifoultout is a relatively small casbah, without really fine interior decoration. Compared to–" Then he broke off short.

The throng around the entrance, made up primarily of Moroccan men in Western clothes who had come out from town to see the dancing, was much more dense than previously. Rick and Bou Hamida managed to push their way through with difficulty, and each took firm hold of one of Dizzy's elbows and towed her along with them.

The scene in the patio had changed, in that everyone had become more relaxed. The musicians were grinning and tapping their feet as they played, and most of the tourists had joined the dancers in clapping to the increased tempo. Across the room Dizzy could see Louella, completely caught up in the rhythm, swaying from side to side and patting her palms together in unison with the dancing women, who smiled at her whenever they turned in her direction.

As before, the music broke off abruptly and rather dissonantly, and the dance stopped. But this time the dancer at the head of the line consulted with a young woman who was apparently the tour director for *Le Groupe*, and she in turn persuaded several of the younger women in her party to join the circle and try to follow the dance.

This effort resulted in great hilarity among the musicians as well as the guests, but gradually the line was re-formed with half a dozen tourists interspersed among the barefoot, brightly dressed Moroccans. Then Dizzy, who had been vainly trying to make her way toward Louella, stopped in surprise and amusement. Two sturdy native musicians had pulled the stout woman to her feet, and with her face wreathed in smiles she was rubbing shoulders with two giggling dancers.

A delightful and touching pantomime ensued. The Moroccans nodded at Louella encouragingly and admired a gold bracelet she was wearing by fingering it. Then they took her hands in theirs and indicated the step they would be doing next. When the drums began to beat once more, someone started a song with a repetitive phrase that Louella, who had a strong musical sense, could follow, and in moments she was not only dancing but singing, as full of zest as the youngest girl on the floor.

All of the Moroccans were delighted. Dizzy could see that while they enjoyed having the other tourists join them, they would always remain strangers, but Louella was welcomed as one of their own. When, in the next interval, she tried out a few of her Arabic phrases, they crowded around her in pleasure. She was the hit of the evening as far as the performers were concerned.

Dizzy and Rick, with Bou Hamida beside them, watched from the background as the fun became more informal. The troupe of women, after accepting enthusiastic applause with modest bows, retired to the courtyard, but the musicians remained and played for everyone who wanted to continue to dance. Louella was whirled around by one partner after another. Light on her feet in spite of her bulk, she was obviously having the time of her life. Dizzy saw her stepping around the floor with the tall, dark leader of the band, with the Englishman in tweeds, and with the Berber driver of the tourist bus. She hadn't looked their way once.

But for their own sobering encounter with Dr. Harding's assistant Dizzy and Rick might have relaxed and joined the crowd whirling around the patio, doing every kind of step from the very latest to an old-fashioned schottische. Now, however, they were again aware of the urgency of their quest, and the spirit of jollity that had infected the crowd eluded them.

Finally, with a roll of drums, the musicians escorted the tourists out to their bus, and Louella at last looked around for her two young charges. When she recognized Bou Hamida she came over at once. "I don't see so well from a distance but I thought it was you," she said, then looked puzzled. "Why aren't you where the professor said for you to be?"

Bou Hamida repeated his earlier explanation, and Louella seemed both satisfied and sobered. "We'd best get off to bed right now," she decided, "if we want to get any rest at all." Once more she was the competent duenna; the frolicsome high-stepper had disappeared.

The last obstinate stars were fading from the sky when Dizzy crept downstairs and tiptoed across the tiled patio to the courtyard, where Rick was wiping off the windshield of the car. Louella was right behind her, shivering in the chill morning air, all of last night's gaiety drained away by the mission that lay ahead.

Quietly they started off, down the winding hill and on to the empty highway, each of them fighting the depression that comes with untimely arising, each of them wishing that the sun would hurry to replace the cold gray light.

Ouarzazate was empty. Not a donkey or a camel appeared on the streets. Not a man stirred. "This place gives me the creeps," Rick said.

"How did you sleep?" Dizzy asked with a yawn.

"Little."

"I slept real well," said Louella from the back seat.

"If there were snakes I didn't mind them, I was that tired."

"You should have been, cavorting around like a teenager," Rick scolded. "Boy, that was a free-for-all at the end, a regular bacchanalia."

"Not a bacchanalia. The Arabs don't drink wine," Dizzy corrected him.

"I even saw you dancing with the bus driver," Rick continued, ignoring the interruption. "How did he get into the act?"

"There's no law against *anybody* dancing that I know of," said Louella with a sniff. "You don't have to act so high and mighty about such things, Patrick."

Rick subsided into silence, allowing time for Louella's ruffled feelings to cool, and Dizzy sat hugging her arms and watching the sun come up as the character of the country began to change.

The road was following the course of a riverbed, dry except for interlacing rivulets that wandered in the broad gravelly waste. Date palms, tamarisks, and almond groves straggled along the banks, forming a long oasis of green. The map showed they were driving through the valley of the Oued Dadès, a narrow rope of land which led out into the Sahara like a lifeline through a sea of sand.

On either side of the road roses grew as thick as crabgrass on a suburban lawn. In full bloom, the petals of the flowers were being gathered by scores of women. "So this is where they get all the rose water from," Rick muttered, while Dizzy refrained from commenting that the spreading fields of color looked like fairyland.

Traffic began to appear. Burros piled high with red and white conical baskets, donkeys laden with open bags of rock salt sparkling like crystal, veiled women bent under loads of garden produce—all seemed to be on their way to market. As the sun rose higher the traffic increased. A young boy trotted along with decorated leather bellows slung on his shoulders like Joseph's cloak of many colors. A camel being crowded by its spindle-shanked offspring curled its lip at the passing car, and throngs of pedestrians walking in the center of the road moved patiently out of the way. Rick slowed down for a bridge, then drove through the village of Skoura, where souks were being set up in a walled marketplace, and he was forced to proceed at a careful fifteen miles an hour.

"It's remarkable when you think of it," Rick mused. "Practically everything we see coming to market is made out of what the desert has to offer. These people live in a world of objects made out of baked earth, woven grass, palm wood, and animal skins. There's no metal—or practically none—if you discount empty oil cans."

"Actually, the goathide bags are much more picturesque for carrying water," put in Dizzy. She was learning that while their thoughts might continue to dwell on Felicia or Dr. Harding, it helped ease the tension to indulge in casual conversation along the way.

A few miles after bisecting the village the road along the Dadès straightened out again and a scene burst upon her eyes that needed no effort for her to appreciate. On either side of the river, as far as the eye could reach, one huge casbah after another raised its crenellated walls to the sky.

Even Louella gasped at the impressive sight, and Rick gave a long, low whistle. "These must be the *ksour* Pop talks about," he mused.

"*Ksour?*" Dizzy repeated the strange word questioningly.

"Fortified villages," Rick explained. "The singular is *ksar*." If he sounded slightly condescending it was probably unintentional. "Most of them are in ruins now, but can't you imagine the days when the nomads came in here with their camel trains and traded with the farmers barricaded behind those walls?"

Reaching out of the red earth like extensions of the land itself the *ksour* pushed their battlements into the blue. Roofs rose, one above the other, like pyramids of building blocks, their walls pierced by windows covered with beautiful wrought-iron shields, their towers surrounded by deeply cut fortifications. Dizzy began to count the casbahs as they passed and toted up thirteen before she tired of the game. How sad, she thought, that these glorious buildings had lost their reason for being. Everything that made Morocco so marvelous was here: brilliant colors beneath a blazing sun, the smell of the desert, and the remnants of a mysterious life that somehow had managed to survive in a wilderness setting.

Rick drove on rapidly, and the hours passed. The Fiat was slowed down once more by a few miles of construction, but the *réparation* wasn't nearly as extensive as the service station attendant had predicted. They left the river and drove through a flat, stony desert for three quarters of an hour, and then came into sight of Tinerhir, nestled in the foothills of the Atlas off to the left.

With a sigh of relief, Rick murmured, "I think we're going to make it at last." Dizzy, however, wasn't quite so optimistic. The address of Bou Hamida's cousin was the only clue they had to Dr. Harding's whereabouts, and once more a door could open only to be slammed shut.

"Let's see that address," Dizzy proposed.

Rick handed her his wallet, empty of currency. "It's in there somewhere, among the other cards."

This was Dizzy's first experience of going through a young man's personal effects. There was a Shell credit card, a Massachusetts driver's license, the telephone number of a girl named Deirdre, an advertisement of a tobacconist over which was scrawled the word "pipes," and the name of a New York bookstore. There was a dog-eared ticket for a Car Wash, an unused press pass for a Dartmouth-Harvard football game, and finally the white slip with Bou Hamida's cousin's name and address written on it in a neat, completely vertical hand.

"Abdou Mokhtar," Dizzy read. "Gorge de Todra." She frowned. "That doesn't sound like a street. It sounds like—"

"Sure, I know. A gorge," Rick interrupted. "So can't a guy live in a chasm? I bet those hills ahead are full of them."

"Anything to make things a little more difficult," Dizzy groaned.

"What did you say?"

"Nothing."

"You did, too."

The strain was telling on Rick, as both Dizzy and Louella could see. They looked at one another without speaking, but they communicated nevertheless. This was a time when a man's short temper had to be endured. Dizzy put the various impedimenta back in the wallet and handed it over. She kept Bou Hamida's card.

Rick grunted and stuffed his property into his slacks pocket. His eyes were narrowed against the sun and he was pushing the little car to the limit of its speed.

Ten

It wasn't necessary to ask directions to the Hotel du Sud in Tinerhir. It was situated on the only hill in town, and behind it crouched a pink fortress that could have been nothing but a garrison of the French Foreign Legion.

"Any minute," predicted Rick, "Ronald Colman's going to come riding through that gate on an Arabian stallion."

"Who's Ronald Colman?" asked Dizzy.

"Don't you ever look at television?" Rick asked in reply. "He's an old-time movie actor who was always cast as Beau Geste or one of those types."

"He was wonderful," put in Louella reminiscently. "I recollect how all us girls in West Virginia used to write Hollywood for his picture and pin it up on our bedroom walls."

Shifting to low, Rick crawled up a long driveway to stop between a converted *ksar* and a modern annex built in a hollow square around a swimming pool. Dizzy caught a glimpse of a couple in bathing suits breakfasting at an umbrella-shaded table and couldn't help but feel envious. How relaxed they looked; how free from care.

Louella, stiff from the four-hour drive, followed Dizzy and Rick up the hotel steps slowly. "Not that I expect to get any news of Pop," Rick was saying, "but at least we can find out how to get to the Todra Gorge."

The lobby was dark after the brilliant morning sunlight, and things seemed to be in a state of confusion. A great mound of luggage stood near the desk, behind which a handsome young Moroccan and a pretty girl who could have been either English or American were turning the pages of a big ledger.

Porters were hurrying in and out with boxes and file cases, rope-tied cartons, and even a small steamer trunk. "Looks like moving day," commented Dizzy as she blinked to adjust her eyes to the gloom, because this wasn't tourist baggage that was being carried hither and yon.

"That's just what it is," said the girl behind the desk, glancing up with a smile. "You're Americans, aren't you? I'm from Montclair, New Jersey. I came over here with the Peace Corps a year ago."

Dizzy's and Rick's surprise was only equaled by their delight at encountering someone who could speak English. "But—" Rick faltered, "you weren't here last night."

The girl shook her head. "We've only just arrived." Then she turned proudly to the young Moroccan. "This is my husband, Allal ben Salah, the new manager of this hotel."

No wonder she's proud of him, Dizzy was thinking as she acknowledged Mr. ben Salah's bow and watched him shake hands courteously with Rick. Seldom had she seen such a prepossessing young man. His black hair was thick and shining, his face tanned and lean, and his eyes unexpectedly blue rather than brown. Instead of the ubiquitous jellaba he was wearing a dark Western suit, well pressed and immaculate.

"Good morning," he said in impeccable English. "Is there anything we can do for you?"

Rick quickly explained their errand. No, the ben Salahs had not heard of a Dr. Patrick Harding, nor did a consultation with the outgoing manager or an examination of the register show that the scientist had passed through here. Yes, it was easy to direct Rick and Dizzy to the Todra Gorge, although naturally they couldn't say just where Abdou Mokhtar lived. From the top of the hotel steps Mr. ben Salah proceeded to point out the road they must follow.

"Is it far?" Rick asked.

"Not at all. You can drive it in half an hour. But sometimes it's difficult. You have to ford the river at several places."

Rick looked at Louella dubiously. "You'd better stay here," he suggested. "You can have a rest and eat a decent breakfast. We should be back shortly after ten o'clock."

To this Louella was quite agreeable, because it promised to be a long day. As Dizzy and Rick started off they saw her walking sedately in the direction of the dining room, which stretched along the rear of the lobby behind curtained glass doors.

The Fiat seemed very much lighter without Louella's hundred and ninety pounds weighing down the back seat. It jumped like a jackrabbit at Rick's pressure on the gas pedal, and sped down the hill up which it had crawled so painfully.

There was no possibility of getting lost, because only one road, a narrow earthen track, snaked its way toward the canyon through groves of palm trees and occasional riverside truck gardens.

The trail was rough, twisting in and out at the foot of sheer cliffs as straight and deep as knife wounds in the body of the plateau. To pass the time, Dizzy got out the guidebook and learned that in places the red rock walls of the Todra Gorge rose to well over a thousand feet. This abyss apparently separated the High Atlas range from the Djebel Sarro and, in a smaller way, was the same kind of geological accident that had produced the Grand Canyon of the Colorado.

Rick listened to this information inattentively. He was frowning again, and sitting hunched over the wheel as though he were riding a bronco rather than driving a car. "I hope to heck this Mokhtar character knows where Pop's gone," he said gloomily.

"Suppose he doesn't speak either French or English?" This was Dizzy's chief worry.

"We'll take him back to the hotel and let ben Salah quiz him," Rick replied. "While we're hoping, let's hope he's home."

"He's *got* to be home." Dizzy spoke forcefully. She couldn't endure the thought of another disappointment. Since they were passing an occasional mud house nestled into the narrow strip of land along the winding riverbank she asked, "Shouldn't we stop soon and inquire?"

Rick nodded, and slowed down beside a husky farm girl carrying a bundle of green grass balanced on her head. Black eyes looked suspiciously from over the nose veil that concealed the lower part of the girl's face, and she started to walk faster, ignoring Rick's attempt to question her.

"I think she's frightened," Dizzy said. "We'd better try asking a man."

"It'll be the neatest trick of the week if we find one that speaks anything but a Berber dialect."

"All we need is one who can read," said Dizzy, fingering Bou Hamida's card, with its neat script. Then she looked dismayed. "Aren't we stupid! We should have asked him to write his cousin's name in Arabic."

Rick groaned. "You're so right. This is likely to be a wild goose chase." He rounded a bend in the road, muttered, "Oops!" and pulled up short on the edge of a rushing stream. "This must be one of the fords. Looks bumpy."

"Are those rocks under there? And where does all the water come from?" Dizzy asked.

"The mountains, sweetie, the mountains." Rick began to ease the car forward in low gear, and Dizzy felt a sideways rocking motion, then a decided jolt. If one of those rocks were sharp enough it could blow a tire. But Rick kept his foot steady, and with a lurch and a crunching spray of gravel they reached the opposite bank.

"Good boy," Dizzy said admiringly.

"That's only the first one. They get tougher as we go along," predicted Rick, but nevertheless he looked pleased.

The next ford was indeed more difficult, and the Fiat lodged on a boulder in midstream and stuck there. "Move over here and step on the gas when I tell you to." Rick was pulling off his loafers and socks as he spoke. Then he rolled up his trousers and opened the door of the car, just as two little boys, big-eyed with curiosity, appeared from behind a clump of oleanders.

"Hi," Rick said as he stepped into the stream and sloshed around to the back of the car. Bending, he put a shoulder against the rear and shouted, "Give her the gun, Diz!"

The Fiat lurched forward momentarily, then settled back, while the Arab children came running through the water and pushed against either end of the rear bumper. They were so slight and frail that their efforts were totally useless, but nevertheless Rick grinned encouragingly and pretended they were a great help.

Leaning out of the car window, Dizzy called, "Want to try again?" Then, from around the bend in the road, she saw a panniered donkey appearing. This meant that help couldn't be far behind. Actually, it was not one man but two who put their shoulders to work alongside Rick. Good-naturedly they pushed and shoved, rocked and bullied the little car until it was persuaded to climb the opposite bank. Then they proudly refused Rick's offer of money. This was all in the day's work.

At the last minute Dizzy remembered to show them the card bearing Mokhtar's name and address, but they shook their heads and glanced at one another in such consternation that she realized neither could read. They pointed ahead, however, in a decisive sort of way. Apparently rescue of another sort was close at hand.

Five minutes later this guess proved correct. Beside a low stone building set close to the road a Volkswagen was pulled up, and in a souvenir shop glimpsed through the open door two women and a man could be seen inspecting brass teapots and trays.

Hopefully, Dizzy approached the proprietor and presented her card. Although he glanced at her curiously he was immediately helpful. "*Ah, oui! Continuez tout droit,*" he said.

"*Merci. Merci beaucoup!*" Dizzy hurried out of the shop and called to Rick, "Straight ahead!"

"He recognized the name?" asked Rick as Dizzy slipped back into the seat beside him.

"At once." Recalling the expression in the proprietor's eyes she added, "I think we should be a little cautious. We don't know anything about this fellow, after all."

"He's Bou Hamida's cousin. Isn't that enough?"

"I'm not so sure. My grandmother had a cousin who was a bootlegger."

"Well, that's one thing you may be sure this Mokhtar lad isn't," Rick replied with a grin.

The road, far from straight, was narrowing to a rocky trail. It led into an invisible cleft in the saffron cliffs, and after a third easy ford the river became a mere trickle of water in a bed of gravel and rock. It was inconceivable to Dizzy that over the centuries such a stream could have carved out this deep gorge.

By the minute the country became wilder and more desolate. No children played here. Not a bird sang. No tree thrust up green leaves to the distant heavens. Even the sun found the chasm difficult to penetrate.

"We're reaching the end of the road," Rick said. Then Dizzy pointed ahead. A low building fashioned crudely of local stone cemented with *pisé*, sun-baked mud, huddled at the foot of a precipice. On the uneven rock terrace before it a couple of rusty metal tables were surrounded by chairs painted in gaudy reds and yellows, and on the side of the building was posted a fading Coca-Cola sign. The overall effect was both dismal and disreputable.

Rick parked the car on the near side of the river-bed and together he and Dizzy picked their way across on stepping stones made by a series of lethal-looking boulders. "Let me handle this," Rick suggested, and Dizzy could tell by his tone that he disliked the appearance of the place as much as she.

From the door of the café a thin, wiry man emerged, dressed in full gray pantaloons and wearing a dirty white apron. Dizzy scrutinized him. Black hair, brown eyes, heavy eyebrows, long upper lip. As she drew closer she noted a mole on his left cheekbone and the wariness in his eyes. He stood and waited, unsmiling, until Rick asked in French for two glasses of mint tea. Uninvited, he led Dizzy to the nearest table and sat down.

The Arab nodded and withdrew, while Rick muttered, "At least he understands French, but English would be easier."

"You don't think Droopy Drawers is Mokhtar?" Dizzy asked in an undertone.

"Why not? There doesn't seem to be anyone else around."

"I don't like his looks," Dizzy confessed.

Rick shrugged. "He's not very pretty, but if he knows where Pop is that's all that counts."

At this point the Moroccan, now wearing a red fez

set at a cocky angle on his head, returned with a tray containing a teapot and two smeary glasses. Dizzy sniffed mistrustfully as the aroma of mint reached her nostrils. Once burned, she thought to herself, twice shy.

Rick, however, was leaning back in his chair as though he were quite relaxed. "Is your name Mokhtar?" he asked.

The wary eyes narrowed, showing that the fellow understood. He gave a short nod. "Abdou Mokhtar."

"How much English do you speak?"

"How much you want?" The voice was surly.

"I want enough to know whether you've seen my father in the past two days. An American—Dr. Harding? You know him, yes?"

The Moroccan kept his eyes fixed on Rick, ignoring Dizzy. "Why?"

"Your cousin, Bou Hamida, said you were to find Dr. Harding a jeep to take into the desert."

Mokhtar shook his head. "No jeep in Tinerhir."

"Then where did my father go?"

The answer was a shrug.

"Didn't he *say* where he was going?"

"Maybe hotel."

"He's not in the hotel and he never has been," said Rick, sitting up straight. "If there was a change in plan he was to leave a message with you for Bou Hamida. This is important, Mokhtar." Rick's voice had acquired an edge. "We've got to find him, fast." He shoved back his chair and leaned on the table with both palms, thrusting out his chin pugnaciously.

The Arab backed away a couple of paces. "No message. I have note for Bou Hamida," he said.

"Let's see it." Rick's voice was still sharp.

Mokhtar shook his head. "For Bou Hamida," he repeated stubbornly.

"Look here!" Rick shouted, thoroughly angry. "I'm Patrick Harding, understand? Bou Hamida sent us to you so we could find my father. There's been a—an accident—and we've got to reach him." Dizzy could tell that Rick was barely able to refrain from saying it was a matter of life and death.

Still Mokhtar was reluctant. "You say he send you. But how do I know?"

Dizzy spoke up. "Can you recognize your cousin's handwriting?" she asked, picking up the card that had been lying on the table. "Here. Look at this."

Mokhtar took the small card suspiciously, as though it might develop fangs and bite him. Then he squinted and examined the upright script for several seconds. It was a space of time during which Dizzy's heart fell. Suppose, like so many Moroccans, he was illiterate? Then she comforted herself with the thought that he had some knowledge of both French and English, and therefore must be better educated than most.

Impatiently, Rick asked, "Well?"

The wary eyes of the Moroccan turned calculating. "How much you pay?"

"Pay?" Rick bellowed. "I'll be doggoned–" He paused as he felt Dizzy's hand on his arm.

"Let's make a bargain, and once we have the note, let's get out of here."

"You're the one with the money," returned Rick sulkily. He looked like a man about to say, "I'd rather fight than switch."

Dizzy turned to Mokhtar. "Five dirhams," she said.

The man curled his lip, showing yellowed teeth. He didn't bother to reply.

"Ten?" suggested Dizzy, doubling her bid.

"Twenty," said Mokhtar.

It was Dizzy's turn to shake her head. "I haven't got that much," she fibbed.

"Let's see."

"Get the note first." She was surprised at the firmness of her own voice.

Mokhtar seemed to be weighing a decision. Then he turned and shuffled toward the door, his pantaloons billowing, his *babouches* flapping at the heels.

Under cover of the table Dizzy opened her pocketbook and extracted her wallet, quickly shoving a wad of bills into the heel of one of her flats. When Mokhtar returned with an envelope in his hand she was counting out notes and coins on the tabletop. "Twelve dirhams is all I can give you," she said with a gaze as innocent as a Botticelli cherub's. Pushing the money toward him she added, "I'm sorry, but this will have to do."

She saw Rick's muscles tense, and she knew that if Mokhtar refused, he would jump him. But suppose the fellow carried a knife? With her most winning smile Dizzy concealed her sudden terror. "Here," she said, and held out a hand for the note.

Still Mokhtar hesitated. "I've got to have it back," he said truculently. "For Bou Hamida. See. Here's his name."

There it was indeed, in Dr. Harding's bold script. He must have scrawled the name hurriedly, because the pen had jabbed through the paper at several points. Could the professor have been angry, Dizzy wondered, or just impatient at one more delay?

"I see." She nodded, aware that the interchange was now between herself and Mokhtar. She felt that her hand had been held out for an aeon, so heavy did it feel.

And then the smooth white envelope was in her grasp. She turned to Rick. "Shall I open it, or will you?"

"You may as well," Rick said, his voice hoarse with anticipation.

Dizzy turned the envelope over and tried to get a finger under the flap, but it was sealed tight, so she had to tear off the end. Her hand trembled as she pulled out a folded sheet of white paper. Then she opened it and gave a shocked moan of despair.

It was completely blank.

Eleven

"Why?" Dizzy asked aloud as the car jolted through the second river ford on its return trip. With an impetuous recoil and a jarring sound it skidded among the rocks and bucked up the shelving bank. "Why would your father do such a thing?"

Rick didn't answer. He was sunk in discouragement too deep for words, and Dizzy could offer him no comfort. She too felt that they had reached the end of the line.

Yet her active brain kept seeking answers to the spoken question: why a blank sheet of paper in an envelope bearing Bou Hamida's name? Could the message have been written in invisible ink? She couldn't imagine Dr. Harding being so devious. Anyway it was too late to make a test.

Dizzy discarded invisible ink as just too silly. Then why leave the envelope at all? To confuse the situation, perhaps—but what situation? Could Dr. Harding have suspected that Mokhtar was in the pay of the Communists, and might use knowledge of where the expedition had gone to American disadvantage?

This scheme seemed to make a little more sense, because certainly Mokhtar was willing to do anything for money, no matter how insignificant the sum. It was also possible that he might have steamed open the envelope and discovered the route Dr. Harding planned to take, then substituted another sheet of paper.

A neat answer, certainly, but one that Dizzy's keen memory rejected. The envelope and the stationery inside had been matching, and of a type that would never be found in southern Morocco. Even cursory examination had registered this on her mind.

Then why leave the envelope at all?

To express his annoyance at Bou Hamida because he had failed to arrive on time? Again this seemed a childish thing to do. Besides, it was important for the Arabs to catch up with the rest of the team. Speed was essential. This had been stressed all along.

Dizzy's thoughts returned to the afternoon the Land Rover had been packed with the prospecting equipment. Two men had accompanied Dr. Harding, two experienced Berbers who apparently knew the desert and the job they had been hired to do. Could one of these men be a traitor? Had he been the one to steam open the envelope and substitute the blank paper? It was a possibility.

On closer inspection, however, it seemed most unlikely. Dr. Harding's handwriting on the envelope had been conspicuously hasty and annoyed. Annoyed at the failure to find a jeep waiting as promised? Probably, but the jabs of the pen indicated something further: that the enclosure of the blank sheet of paper had been deliberate.

But why? Dizzy went back to the beginning and tried a different tack. Suppose she attempted to add up all the incidents of the past few days and see what sum she could reach?

First there was the drugged mint tea. Then there was Felicia's disappearance. This addition was easy. The two circumstances were joined the minute a kidnapping was suspected.

Next there was the disappearance of the slip containing Mrs. Harding's Paris address. Either Felicia had picked it up and taken it along with her to the souks or—and this seemed more likely—there was an enemy of American interests within the Harding household itself. Ruling out Louella, who was left but Ali, Abdul, and the two undergardeners, whose names Dizzy didn't know?

In fourth place Dizzy put the Countess de Redier's reluctance to go to the police. All along this had bothered her, and in view of their present straits it seemed doubly suspicious. Of course Bou Hamida had backed her up when he had learned about Felicia's disappearance. But suppose the Countess and Bou Hamida were in cahoots?

Accustomed, from childhood, to separating the Goodies from the Baddies, this led Dizzy along a new line of conjecture. Suppose, together, this oddly assorted pair were working against both the Americans and the Moroccan government?

Would this be a reason for the latest peculiar discovery—the non-letter left by Dr. Harding? Only if he had somehow discovered their treachery, but in that case wouldn't he have headed straight back for Marrakech?

"Rick, would your father attempt to go into the desert alone—without Bou Hamida, I mean? He's got two men with him in the Land Rover, along with all the equipment. Could the three of them do the job?"

"I doubt it," Rick said gloomily.

"But you're not sure?"

"What are you driving at, anyway?"

"To tell you the truth, I don't know," Dizzy confessed. Her thoughts were glancing against one another like swaying crystal prisms. She was seeing Bou Hamida's smiling face as he entered the Casbah of Tifoultout, the smile erased by concern when he first saw Rick. She was hearing him urge them on at all possible speed when he learned of Felicia's disappearance. She could hardly suggest to Rick that his father's assistant might be suspect. Not when Bou Hamida was trying his best to help.

At the hotel Louella was settled in a comfortable chair awaiting their return stoically. When they told her the dismaying news she had an immediate answer. "We'd best get straight back home."

"Not until we've had something to eat," Rick replied. "Those leftover sandwiches were O.K. five hours ago, but they're not going to last me all day."

"Perhaps the hotel would pack us a picnic lunch," Dizzy suggested. "Shall I ask when I order breakfast?"

Young Mrs. ben Salah, immediately solicitous, said of course this could be arranged. Also, since it was only ten thirty the kitchen was still serving breakfast, and with persuasion could probably produce an omelet for two along with *café au lait* and hard rolls.

Dizzy and Rick, followed by Louella, who had become bored with her own company, repaired to a dining-room table, their spirits at a low ebb. Rick had brought a road map from the car and he began to study it moodily, trying to figure out what route his father might have taken into the desert from Tinerhir.

"Pop's heading for a region almost due south of here," he said to Dizzy after a while. "It's sand-dune country, where the boundary between Morocco and Algeria has been in dispute for years. All this map shows is a wide gray ribbon marked Frontier Undefined."

Dizzy toyed with a salt cellar and said, "It sounds sort of dangerous."

"Well, Pop didn't act as though this trip would be a picnic," Rick replied. "And I'm sure he counted heavily on hiring a second Land Rover or jeep for Bou Hamida and the workers he's bringing along."

"Isn't your father trying to stake out his claim—if the ground shots show any likely pools of oil—before the Soviets beat him to it?"

"That's right."

"Then how could he reach the drilling site fastest?"

"Well," said Rick, examining the map once more, "he could go from here to Erfoud and then into the desert, or if he was still hoping to pick up a jeep he could cut across to Zagora on a pretty rough track—"

"Zagora?" asked Louella as though she savored the taste of the strange name on her tongue. "That's where the bus driver out at the casbah had been—Zagora."

"That fellow you were casting sheep's eyes at?" Rick accused her.

"We had some conversation while we were dancing," Louella said stiffly. "Or do you think there's harm in talking, Patrick Harding? Tell me that?"

"You mean *Le Groupe* had just come from Zagora to Ouarzazate?" Dizzy was interested. "Louella, you didn't ask the driver if he'd seen an American in a Land Rover?"

" 'Course I did, Miss Deborah. Do you think I'm stupid? He'd seen an American, all right, but it wasn't the professor. This man's name was Mr. Wheel."

"Mr. what?" asked Dizzy.

"Mr. Wheel. That's what he said. He heard a man call him."

"Well, that's disappointing," muttered Rick as if this were par for the course. He returned to squinting at the road map between sips of coffee, but Dizzy found herself repeating silently Mr. Wheel, Mr. Wheel, and thinking it strange—

Suddenly she gave a startled cry. "Rick, it's your father!"

"Mr. Wheel? Don't be—"

"Not Mr. Wheel, Mr. H-u-i-l-e. That's what his helpers call him, I'll bet. Mr. Oil, in French! Why, it's obvious!"

Rick put down the map and stared at Dizzy with dawning comprehension and a degree of admiration. "You might have something there," he admitted. "How far's Zagora from here?"

"You've got the map," Dizzy said, but went around the table to look over his shoulder.

"As the crow flies it's not very far," Rick said. "Look here."

"You'd best remember we are not crows," Louella interjected, but she seemed more cheerful than previously, perhaps because she had contributed some information of value. In fact, she smiled at her own attempt at a joke.

"There's a broken line from here to here," Rick was saying. "That means a track. Let's ask the ben Salahs. Maybe they'll know whether we can get across in the Fiat." Recovering his former energy he jumped to his feet. "Come on!"

Mr. ben Salah was behind the desk along with the former manager, a sour-looking fellow who was apparently showing him the ropes. The older man seemed to resent the interruption, but the young Moroccan was affable and interested. "I'm sorry to tell you," he said in answer to Rick's question, "but you can't possibly cross the *piste* in your little car. You'll have to go the long way around."

"You mean almost back to Ouarzazate?" Rick groaned. "That's one hundred and fifteen kilometers plus one hundred and seventy-two."

Mr. ben Salah nodded. "And the last fifty are rugged going," he said, "but if you leave right away you should be able to get there by sunset."

"Let's go," said Dizzy.

Louella assented by murmuring, "Thank goodness for the picnic lunch."

Packed in three cardboard boxes, it had just been put on the counter by a servant from the kitchen. The bill was totaled and paid. Then they were off. Off in a cloud of dust, which enfolded the car in a gritty cloak, becoming hotter and more disagreeable as the day advanced. Every two hours Dizzy and Rick exchanged stints at the wheel, and by mid-afternoon, dripping with perspiration, they were driving through the Draa Valley. "I feel like a piece of soggy eggplant dipped in brown sugar," Dizzy said. No longer did the *ksour* they passed seem so romantic. Instead, the stones beside the road that marked each passing kilometer attracted her eyes.

Louella was still monumental in the back seat, but she looked like a melting monument, Dizzy decided as she glanced over her shoulder. The cook sat with her eyes closed, her chin resting on her ample bosom, as the car labored on toward Zagora at fifteen miles an hour.

An oasis of locust-ravaged date palms with branches bare as umbrella ribs led to another stretch of stony desert baking under the afternoon sun. Dizzy shrank away from its glare and tried to keep her arms from touching the overheated metal in which she was encased. Never before had she known such discomfort, never such an endless trip. She began to understand why the nomads accompanying occasional camel trains were swathed to the eyes in heavy clothing. The bite of this sun was as fiery as if its rays were focused by a burning glass.

Rick must have been just as wretched, but he was too busy worrying about whether the water in the radiator would boil over to concentrate on his physical state. When the numbers on the kilometer stones finally duplicated those in a satellite countdown, he said with a relieved sigh, "Twenty minutes more and we'll be there."

From the plain ahead rose the mountain called Djebel Zagora, 3,000 feet high. The landmark was a welcome sight indeed, and the three watched it grow with relief that was shared though unspoken.

Still another of the Hotels du Sud that studded the Moroccan Sahara opened its doors to greet them. Rick and Dizzy hurried to the desk and made immediate inquiries. Had an American with a Land Rover and two Berber companions been registered here?

The answer was yes, but after a quick inspection the young people saw that the name Harding did not appear in the book.

"Could you describe this man?" Rick asked the clerk in French.

"*Pourquoi?*"

"If it's my father we must do our best to reach him," Rick replied. "There is a family emergency."

Dizzy could understand only snatches of the following conversation, but she gathered that the desk clerk was able to satisfy Rick that there was no mistake. Dr. Harding and his helpers had indeed stopped over here, but why the professor had decided to travel under an assumed name was anyone's guess.

"When did the American leave?" Rick asked after being told that the party had proceeded southward.

"Yesterday morning, very early."

Rick gulped, and Dizzy could have wept. "You're positive?"

The clerk nodded. "I remember distinctly, because he made certain to get his bill paid and start off before

Le Groupe came down for breakfast. I've never seen a man in such a hurry."

Rick turned to Dizzy ruefully. "He doesn't know Pop," he said in English. " 'Haste makes waste' isn't in his lexicon. He believes haste makes sense."

Haste makes sense. An interesting idea, Dizzy thought as she stood by while Rick thanked the desk clerk for the information and arranged for rooms. What had happened along the route to accelerate Dr. Harding's plans and cause him to leave Zagora without his full complement of assistants? Had he tried to hire a jeep here as he had in Tinerhir? Had he tried and once more failed?

Louella and the young people were escorted to meagerly furnished chambers looking out over the endless desert. With *Le Groupe* gone it was obvious the place was almost empty. The deep South was territory that attracted only the most intrepid tourists in summer.

After showers all three revived somewhat. The sun had gone down and with it the sting left the day's heat. Louella decided to rest until the eight o'clock dinner hour, but perplexity and disappointment made Dizzy restless. "Let's take a walk," she proposed to Rick when she found him drinking a coke in the downstairs bar.

He agreed readily enough. "After thirteen hours jackknifed into that car I need some exercise."

Outside the light was soft, and every street led to the medina, which always came alive in the early evening. Blue people, as the indigo-robed Tuaregs were called, had come in from the desert with camel caravans. Nomads were bargaining for the few needs the souks must provide—tea and spices, rock sugar and salt. Tantalizing veiled women of indeterminate age shopped in the fruit markets, and on the hard-packed earth of the square a "doctor" sat cross-legged, a chart showing the human body's most vulnerable organs gathering dust in front of him, while a wooden pointer lay across his knees and potential customers limped blindly by.

In spite of herself Dizzy was fascinated by the kaleidoscopic throng, but Rick had not yet given up seeking his father. "From here on," he said, "there's only the oasis of Mhamid. Then it's gazelle country and open desert. But if we had a jeep—"

"It seems pretty obvious by now that there's no jeep available, and even if there were, we couldn't haul Louella into the desert. She's been a dandy sport so far, but the only thing that's keeping up her courage is that tomorrow we'll be heading for home."

"I could go on alone."

Rick was talking at random, and Dizzy knew it, but she only asked, "How are you at riding camels? Or are those creatures with one hump called dromedaries?" She was trying to visualize the picture on the cardboard date cartons that always appeared in Connecticut at Thanksgiving and Christmas. Unexpectedly she was swept by a wave of homesickness. "If I see one more man on a donkey I'm going to scream," she said under her breath.

But the next man she saw on this common beast of burden gave the lie to this remark. With the help of a small boy a Moroccan patriarch who could have made two of Louella was mounting a sturdy animal that looked equally oversized. The man was not only huge; he was handsome. Eyes sparkling with intelligence, curly white hair bushing from under a stylish turban, and an equally curly beard that Santa Claus might have envied made him outstanding in a country of handsome men. He was wearing a jellaba of unusual design, which led Rick to say, "I wonder if he's a Muslim priest?"

The man was settling himself astride the donkey rather than sidesaddle as many Moroccan peasants rode. He grinned at the boy who had helped him, tossed him a coin, and turned the donkey toward the far side of the square. Coming along at a fast clip in Dizzy's direction, he spotted her blond hair and raised his eyebrows with interest. "Hello!" he called genially as he trotted past.

Dizzy was amused. "He spoke to me in English!"

"Could be the only word he knows."

Dizzy stood looking after the stout figure and said, "Somehow I doubt it. I wonder what he's doing in Zagora. He looks out of place."

Twelve

The patriarch looked even more out of place in the hotel dining room, where he was one of two guests being served when Louella, restored by her long nap, preceded Dizzy and Rick to a table.

In a dark corner sat a Frenchman with the look of a traveling salesman, eating abstractedly while he made notations in a small black book. By contrast the white-bearded Arab was obviously a person of importance. He commanded even more attention than Louella from the hotel staff.

At each stopover it had been Louella who was treated with special courtesy by the servants. Her authoritative bulk, added to her pleasant disposition and her rich brown color, pleased the Moroccans and made them eager to help her out of the car and commandeer her luggage. Dizzy and Rick were left to follow along behind.

Tonight all was as usual. Louella was seated first in

the best position on the sofa that served as a banquette. Dizzy edged in beside her, but Rick had to make do with an uncomfortable chair on the opposite side of the table, with his back to the room.

Again Dizzy's blond head caught the elderly Moroccan's attention. He smiled and nodded in her direction, while Louella, on the *qui vive* for possible trouble, whispered, "Who's that?"

"I don't know. We passed in the medina and he waved to me. Hasn't he a nice smile?"

The waiter, who was standing by ready to take an order, became aware of the direction of Louella's glance. "*C'est une personnalité, un imam de Rabat*," he told her as though his hotel was honored to have such a visitor.

Rick translated. "An *imam* is a kind of religious leader, a very well-educated man."

"He looks like Santa Claus," Louella decided in an undertone when the waiter had left. Then she turned her attention to the business at hand, the plans that must be made for the next day.

Both she and Dizzy had reached the same conclusion. They must get back to Marrakech as fast as possible. Only Rick continued to hope that he might still catch up with his father. Several inquiries concerning the availability of desert transportation had met with no success; but nevertheless he clung tenaciously to the notion of going out into the Sahara.

"That you will not do, Patrick. Now hear me. This skylarkin' is over, and we drive straight home tomorrow and telephone King Hassan if necessary. Or even the President of the United States." Louella sounded very firm.

Rick slouched in his chair, sunk in gloom, but he didn't try to argue. Dizzy felt that further dissuasion was unnecessary. He was bound to realize, sooner or later, that any such idea was an impossible dream.

Personally, she was fighting off a feeling of panic. When she thought of Felicia her flesh crawled, and when she counted the kilometers between here and Marrakech she realized that tomorrow would be another nightmare of heat and dust. With luck, the best they could hope for would be to end at the beginning —to arrive at the point of their departure three days before.

Louella's nightly phone calls to Ali at the Hardings' villa had elicited little. The children's mother had not yet phoned and Miss Felicia had not returned. The Countess de Redier had been to the house several times, but although she went through the mail each day there were no letters of concern to the family, or so she said.

Until now Dizzy had tried her level best to keep Rick's and Louella's spirits up, but tonight she shrank from the task. The service in the dining room was slow, and the *couscous*, a lamb stew with vegetables and semolina, was mediocre. Only Louella managed to finish the food on her plate.

While the table was being cleared the bearded *imam*, a glass of mint tea in his hand, walked across the room and bowed politely. "May I join you?" he asked in English with an Oxford accent.

"We'd be delighted," Dizzy said as Rick stood up to shake hands. Any diversion at this point would be welcome, because disappointment had sent all three of them into a funk.

Introductions were made, and the dignitary, whose name was Mourad Bennani, mentioned that he was surprised to see American tourists in Zagora at this time of year.

"And we're surprised to meet someone who speaks English," Dizzy replied.

"Ah, but I also speak French and several Arabic dialects," the *imam* replied with a warm smile. "You see, I am a Koranic scholar. Languages are important to me, and I seize on a chance to practice my English whenever possible."

"You've been to Mecca, haven't you, sir?" Rick asked.

"Yes, I have made the pilgrimage twice."

"Then shouldn't we call you Hadji?"

"If you like. I am a *hadji*." Mourad Bennani sounded both pleased and slightly amused. "Now tell me," he said, turning to Dizzy, "how are you enjoying Zagora?"

"We've only just arrived," Dizzy replied. She felt no need to explain that their stay would be brief.

"But in the medina you have seen the Tuaregs. Do you know why they're called the Blue Men?"

"Because they wear blue robes and turbans," Dizzy said promptly. "But I expected their skin to be stained blue too."

"Not long ago you would have found it so," Hadji Bennani said. "You see, back in the middle of the nineteenth century some British traders arrived with a shipload of cheap indigo cotton. They sold it to the desert people, who liked the blue-black shine to the fabric, but the dye was obtained from plants grown in the Sudan and the color wasn't fast.

"You had only to touch the stuff to stain your fingers blue, but the Tuaregs enjoyed having the dye rub off on their arms and faces and feet. It was an extra protection against the burning Saharan sun. Today the indigo dye is made chemically, which I consider a pity. To see truly blue-skinned people is becoming a thing of the past."

Louella had been listening quietly. This fine-looking man was obviously so genuine that her mood began to soften. "Patrick's daddy is an American professor," she bragged when she could get an opening.

Dizzy could see that this embarrassed Rick, but the *hadji* was understanding. "Really? At what school?"

"M.I.T.," returned Louella proudly. "That's the Massachusetts Institute of Technology."

Hadji Bennani turned to Rick. "By chance is your

father the scientist who was here a couple of days ago?"

Hesitating, Rick glanced at Dizzy, then decided it was safe to tell the truth. "Yes, we're trying to catch up with him."

"But he has gone into the desert. Mhamid is the last oasis in this valley, and he must have left there by mid-morning yesterday. How unfortunate that the telephone line does not go on."

"You talked to Dr. Harding?" Dizzy asked excitedly.

"We chatted, although I didn't know his name. The desert people call him Mr. Huile—or sometimes Mr. Zoom-zoom, because he travels so fast."

"That's my father," said Rick in a tone of discouragement that overlaid his usual pride. "This is one time I wish he'd been forced to make haste slowly." Then he said, with unconcealed emotion, "It's desperately important to get to him. Isn't there some way—?"

Hadji Bennani shook his head. "To venture into the desert without a caravan of either jeeps or camels would be suicidal for an amateur."

Louella assumed an I-told-you-so expression but kept silent, while Rick tried to argue this stern pronouncement. In return he received a lecture that would have intimidated the bravest of young men. The Sahara was a menace to the inexperienced, a cauldron of swirling sand in the daytime that turned cold as snow at night. Even the nomad Tuaregs respected its authority. Had Rick not noted the *taligmus*—the face veil worn to protect the eyes, lips, and nostrils from the parching glare?

Rick had, and as a matter of fact he was already suffering from sunburn. He subsided, and to Dizzy's relief seemed to accept the inevitable return to Marrakech.

Although he could not have guessed the reason behind Rick's anxiety, Hadji Bennani nevertheless seemed to appreciate the need to reach Dr. Harding. "You could leave your father a message at the hotel desk," he suggested. "He's bound to come back this way."

This seemed to be taking a lot for granted. Puzzled, Dizzy asked, "How can you be sure?"

"Because the professor hired a jeep here and took along a couple of extra laborers as well as a native driver." The *hadji* added, for Rick's benefit, "No wise man would venture into the desert with only one car." Then he smiled and confessed, "I'm a light sleeper, and the early morning racket aroused me. That's why I know so much about who went with your father and exactly when he got off."

Dizzy listened carefully, sorely tempted to pour out the whole tale of Felicia's disappearance to this intelligent and kindly counselor. Yet nothing could be gained, since a desert expedition was patently impossible. At least, she comforted herself, they would leave Zagora with one new piece of information. Dr. Harding had managed to acquire that important second car.

This knowledge was a relief to Rick also. While Dizzy cashed another traveler's check he wrote duplicate notes to his father, one addressed to Dr. Patrick Harding and the other to the pseudonym under which he had been registered. It wasn't necessary to tell the desk clerk that the envelopes were both intended for the same man.

"By the way," he questioned in an afterthought, "is there any message for a Mr. Bou Hamida?"

The clerk checked a number of envelopes. "No sir, sorry sir," he said.

Again a picnic lunch was ordered, and the following morning Dizzy met Louella and Rick at first light. The prospect of the long trip ahead was a dreary one. No longer could the strange country bewitch her with its *ksour* and its oases. She felt beaten and depressed.

Neither Louella nor Rick was talkative on the rough ride to Ouarzazate. Rick was driving, so Dizzy slumped in the front seat and let her mind slide back over the meagre discoveries of the past three days. She could tick them off on the fingers of one hand. First, Bou Hamida's broken axle had caused a serious delay. Second, Bou Hamida's cousin had failed to produce the promised jeep and was apparently a scoundrel who would sell anything for money. Third, Dr. Harding's reaction to this setback was to leave his assistant a message saying exactly nothing and approach his destination from another point. Fourth, at Zagora he had been successful in mounting his expedition properly, and had gone into the desert without either waiting for Bou Hamida or leaving him news of his whereabouts. Fifth, this added up to a certainty that the scientist no longer relied on his assistant. In fact, there was every indication that he distrusted him.

That makes two of us, thought Dizzy, and wondered if Rick had reached the same conclusion. She remembered the smile so quickly wiped from Bou Hamida's face the evening they had encountered him at Tifoultout. But then why had he been so solicitous? Why had he urged them to hurry? Why had he seemed so anxious that they reach Dr. Harding before he vanished into the sands?

Dizzy bit her lip, because she was faced with a contradiction. "Did it ever occur to you," she asked Rick softly, so as not to disturb Louella, who was dozing in the back seat, "that Bou Hamida was terribly anxious to have us find your father and bring him back home?"

"Of course. Why not?" Rick continued to concentrate on the road ahead. "That's what we all hoped for, isn't it?"

"Yes," Dizzy had to admit, but she felt that some facet of the situation was eluding her. She was still pondering the problem when they reached the outskirts of Ouarzazate and began to drive along the now familiar main street.

"We're going to need gas," Rick said, "and we may as well find out when the Chevy took off yesterday."

"Was it only yesterday?" Dizzy sighed. "It seems like a week." Then she straightened up as a ramshackle hotel bearing a Greek name came into sight. "Look, that's the place Bou Hamida must have stayed, and here's the garage he mentioned, remember? Almost next door."

Rick turned in and stopped at the petrol pump, then got out of the car and sauntered over to a mechanic who was lying flat on the ground half under a pick-up truck. Dizzy, whose turn it was to drive, followed him, and stood by while he used a combination of sign language and French to find out what they wanted to know.

First he crouched down and pointed to the truck's rear axle, then made a breaking motion with his hands and said, "*Chevy, hier?*" The fellow seemed to understand, because he repeated the word Chevy and said, "*Vert?*"

"Right," Rick said. "Green. *À quelle heure est-il parti?*"

The mechanic shrugged.

Rick indicated the axle again. "You fix?"

The fellow shrugged again and shook his head, while Dizzy started back toward the Fiat. She wasn't surprised that Rick soon gave up and returned too. "He's seen the Chevy all right, but Hamida must have had it repaired at some other garage. Oh, well, let's get our gas and head for the Tizi N'Tichka. That pass will be a breeze after the Zagora road."

Dizzy hung back. "Rick—"

"Yes?"

"I'd be willing to bet a good deal that Bou Hamida never had a broken axle."

"Now why say a thing like that? This is just the wrong garage, that's all."

"You mean you're not a betting man?" Dizzy prodded. "A Kennedy half dollar says I'm right." She reached into the zippered compartment of her handbag. "I've got one right here."

"Well, I haven't," said Rick. "You're the moneybags on this trip. Boy, we're going to have some fancy accounting to do when we get home."

"You're changing the subject," Dizzy objected. "Do we have a bet or don't we?"

"We have one, for a buck," Rick replied. "Since there are only two other garages in this hick town we ought to get the answer pretty fast."

Dizzy's eyes began to sparkle. "A dollar it is, but I may as well warn you. I'm going to take your money, Rick."

Thirteen

"I don't mind losing a dollar, but how did you guess?" Rick asked twenty minutes later as Dizzy drove out past Tifoultout and along the flat highway that led toward the mountains. He twisted around in the seat, putting one arm along the back so that he could turn from Dizzy to Louella.

The question was difficult to answer. "I sort of had a hunch, that's all," Dizzy replied.

"Well, let's play your hunches from here on in."

"I second that motion," Louella said, "but why would Mr. Hamida tell such a big fib? He always seemed real devoted to the professor. Why, he was at the house all the time."

Rick nodded. "What I don't get is this: Hamida fakes a broken axle so that his part of the team is delayed for another day or so, yet he urges us to get with it and hurry along to Pop as fast as we can." He tugged at an ear thoughtfully. "The two things just don't make sense."

"They most surely don't," Louella acknowledged.

Dizzy didn't answer for several minutes. She was impelled to agree, but there had to be a reasonable answer. "Look at it this way," she proposed. "Bou Hamida wants us to reach Dr. Harding. This is important to him. He wants us to be the ones to tell him Felicia has been kidnapped. Do you agree?"

"Why should *we* be the ones to break the news?" Rick asked. "Why couldn't he?"

"He could, but apparently he didn't want to. Otherwise he wouldn't have been dawdling around in Ouarzazate."

"Do you think he's scared of Pop being sore because he got such a late start?"

"Why start at all, in that case?" Dizzy asked.

"You-all keep asking each other questions that haven't got any answers," complained Louella. "All we got to deal with is some simple facts. Mister Hamida told a lie about the axle. That's the most important thing."

"O.K. Hamida is a liar. So what?" asked Rick. "Pop will fire him, quick as a flash, when he finds out. But it still doesn't bring us any closer to discovering what's happened to Felicia." He pounded a fist angrily on the back of the seat. "That's what's worrying me."

Dizzy didn't take her hands off the wheel, but she had an impulse, hard to restrain, to reach out and cover the fist with her hand. Rick was such a solid character, really, with all the right sorts of emotions. Never did he lose sight of their goal—the rescue of his sister. As the responsible older brother, he was taking this whole affair harder than anyone else.

For the first time Dizzy found herself glad that she was a girl and not a man. So much was expected of the male of the species, from childhood on. He must grow up to be strong. He must not cry when hurt. He must be able to lick the school bully. And as a man he must fight the country's wars, protect his womenkind, provide a living for his family. Why, Rick was expected to be King Arthur and Henry Ford and George Washington, all rolled into one.

Dear Rick. Dizzy wished she had an older brother as concerned for her safety as Rick was for Felicia's. Then she glanced his way and reconsidered. No, she didn't want him for a brother after all. She'd rather have him as a good and growing friend.

"What are you doing, thinking?" Rick asked so unexpectedly that Dizzy was startled.

"Yes." She nodded, flushing. She didn't say about what.

"Well, drop those pearls of wisdom."

Dizzy bit her lower lip. "They'd make a dull thud," she confessed. Yet she was still pursued by the sense of being close to some sort of breakthrough, and as the kilometers rolled away under the wheels of the car she kept reviewing the known facts in her mind.

One thing was clear. If she and Rick had managed to reach Dr. Harding he would have headed straight for home. Suppose Bou Hamida had counted on this? Wouldn't that provide a reason for Felicia's kidnapping? To keep her father from beating the Russians into the desert in a search for oil?

But Bou Hamida wasn't a Russian agent—or was he? "Rick, do you think there's a chance the Communists might have bought Hamida out?"

"Bought him out?"

"Bought his services. The way we bought his cousin Mokhtar's. Maybe it runs in the family, to sell out to the highest bidder. It's a thought."

Rick considered the thought glumly, but Dizzy's mind was dashing ahead. "If we accept that then everything else falls into line," she decided aloud. "Felicia disappears at the first possible opportunity after her father's plans for the drilling expedition are all set. He got off a little faster than anybody expected, but there was still time for us to catch up—or so it seemed. As for Bou Hamida, why go chasing all over the South when he expected us to do the work for him and bring Dr. Harding back? Naturally he would stall in Ouarzazate. That Tinerhir trek is no fun in the summertime."

Both Rick and Louella were listening carefully. "You might have something there," Rick admitted.

While Louella said, "It may be just as well that the professor got away before we caught up. He'd want to beat those Russians, that's for sure." As usual, she was quick to show partiality for her boss.

"Aren't you forgetting that Felicia's being held as a hostage, if this is true?" Rick asked.

"At least hostages aren't likely to get killed," placated Dizzy, unconsciously admitting her secret fear.

Rick raised his eyebrows, but he didn't say anything to disabuse her of this notion. "Your theory would explain why we didn't pass the Chevy on the road," he said after consideration. "But then where would Bou Hamida go?"

"Back to Marrakech, maybe? Suppose he's part of a Communist gang who organized the kidnapping. He's still expecting us to show up with your father in tow. That was the whole point, wasn't it?"

"Hey!" Rick objected. "We don't know it's for real."

"But just let's suppose."

"O.K. So?"

"The minute the drilling trip is off, the kidnappers would be told to release Felicia. But if the Americans can't be stopped in time—then what? What happens to a hostage when her value as security is gone?"

Dizzy had arrived at the same point of no return which Rick had reached earlier. "Let's not think about that," he said gruffly. "One thing's sure. We've got to rescue Felicia before Pop gets back. Otherwise what might happen is anyone's guess."

"You-all must go straight to the Chief of Police the instant we get home," advised Louella from the back seat.

"Cops and robbers," murmured Dizzy as though she were thinking aloud. "Let's try some free association. Where would you hide a big girl with long blond hair if you were on the robbers' side, Rick?"

"Not in Marrakech, that's for sure."

"I agree. Then where?"

Rick shook his head. "This isn't exactly a big country, but it's big enough. Free association's for the birds."

"Well, try some deduction," Dizzy suggested as she lapsed into silence. Again she had the feeling that something had eluded her, something important. If only she could—

"Look up ahead!" said Rick, and Dizzy's thoughts were interrupted by the sight of a large crowd of people converging on a small mud village crouched in the foothills of the mountains. From a sleepy, almost deserted huddle of houses it had become a kaleidoscope of bright color. Striped tents had been erected in the nearby fields and a procession of women in brilliant *monsourrias* was approaching a white-domed building near the side of the road.

"It must be a *moussem,*" Rick exclaimed as Dizzy slowed down. "See, that's a marabout—the tomb of a holy man."

Dizzy nodded. These marabouts appeared at intervals throughout the countryside, and she had been told that many Moroccans revered their local saints as symbols of a permanent link between heaven and earth. But *moussem* was a word new to her. "Is it like a fair?" she asked.

Rick shook his head. "No, there's nothing for sale. It's a celebration on the anniversary of a saint's death. People come from miles around and all day long there is feasting and music and processions, and sometimes a fantasia."

"That sounds like Walt Disney," commented Dizzy as she changed gears and slowed down even more. The road ahead was clogged with traffic. Conveyances of every description, from donkey carts to S.A.T.A.S. buses, were crawling along the narrow highway toward a flat plateau as large as a football field.

"It's just about as fantastic," said Rick, making a play on words. "Actually, fantasia is the Italian name for a game played on horseback. It's really something!"

"This might be a good place to have lunch," suggested Louella.

"It might, at that," agreed Dizzy. "Certainly we're not going to make much time until this road gets cleared."

By now the Fiat had become part of the parade. Hedged in on every side by bicycles, burros, and pedestrians, Dizzy glanced at the speedometer and decided they could have made better time walking. Fortunately the scene was distracting. The procession of women, followed by a gaily dressed horde of children, were chanting to the rhythm of their own hand-clapping, while on the opposite side of the road splendidly caparisoned horses were being readied for the ceremonies to come.

Dizzy was seeing a new side of Morocco—opulence in the midst of the grinding poverty of this insignificant village. "They're Arabian and Berber stallions," Rick said in admiration, "especially trained to charge while their riders stick on, no-handed, yelling and firing guns."

"But is this part of a religious celebration?" Rick's description didn't sound very pious to Dizzy.

"Oh, a *moussem* isn't *all* religious," Rick replied. "After the Muslim rites are over there's singing and dancing and storytellers and strolling players and acrobats. It's like the Djemaa-el-Fna in miniature, with a fantasia thrown in for fun and games."

Dizzy took a closer look at the horses, a company of eight sleek, handsome animals wearing jeweled, sequined, or embroidered saddles of great elegance. Their riders sat the mounts proudly. Dressed in white jellabas and smart white turbans, they cradled long silver-decorated muskets in their arms as they started toward the far end of the field.

"Let's park the car. We may as well have a look," Rick suggested. "It's impossible to break through this mob until the traffic thins out."

A few minutes later Dizzy and Rick were mixing with the crowd of onlookers at the near end of the field. Louella hung back. "I'm right scared of gun play," she admitted.

Dizzy, however, was caught up by the drama. Although the heat was intense and dust rose from the field in pink clouds, she forgot her discomfort as she watched the team of horsemen line up in the distance. At a signal the horses started off at breakneck pace, heading straight for the crowd of which Dizzy and Rick were a part. At a second signal from their leader the horsemen raised their muskets in both hands, then fired as one man, producing a din that echoed down the valley. Their mounts, now at a full gallop, did not falter, and Dizzy shrank back against Rick apprehensively, while the horses skidded to a dead stop inches away from the spectators. Their nostrils were quivering with excitement, but they obeyed their riders and trotted back down the field, docile as lambs.

"They're marvelous!" Dizzy breathed. "I've never seen anything like them!" If Felicia hadn't been in danger she could have stayed here all day.

Rick was equally impressed. "It's pretty remarkable to see a sight like this in an age of jets and satellites," he said as they pushed through the dense throng and made their way slowly back toward the car.

On the outskirts of the crowd storytellers were doing their best to attract listeners, and a pair of acrobats had spotted Louella as a potential customer. One was dressed in the tawdry finery of his trade, but the other was wearing workmen's clothes, and caught Rick's attention. He dropped Dizzy's arm to move closer, then gave a sharp cry of astonishment.

"Ibrahim!"

The acrobat made a quick somersault from his companion's shoulders and landed at Rick's feet. Recognition was instantaneous, and his dark eyes grew troubled. "Mr. Patrick! You shouldn't be here!"

"Neither should you," Rick retorted, grabbing the young man's arm, while Dizzy realized that this must be the Berber from Amizmiz whom Rick and the Countess had gone to fetch. "Where's Bou Hamida?" Rick was asking. "What are you doing halfway back home?"

"I left Hamida in Ouarzazate," Ibrahim replied. His English was heavily accented but quite understandable, and Dizzy remembered that his grandfather had been a famous acrobat who had taught him the language as a child.

"Why?"

"I was hired to go into the desert to do a job. Why should he stall around while I lose two days' pay? I don't like that guy."

The American slang term fell strangely from Berber lips, but Dizzy was too interested to notice. "Where's the other workman who was with you?" she asked.

"He walked out when I did, and went back to Marrakech this morning. I'm broke, so I picked up a lift on a truck and thought I'd try to make a few dirhams for the bus fare on from here."

This explanation sounded straight enough, but Dizzy noticed that Rick still kept a firm grip on Ibrahim's arm.

"Do you know what's happened to my sister?" he asked with narrowed eyes.

"Your sister?" Such surprise couldn't have been faked. "I don't know what you're talking about."

"I don't think he does," said Dizzy as Rick glanced her way. Yet she couldn't be sure, so she sidestepped the subject of the kidnapping and said, instead, "Ibrahim, we agree with you about Bou Hamida. We think he may be working for the Communists and is trying to help the Russians beat the Americans to new oil fields. Now think. Can you remember anything at all suspicious that Bou Hamida said?"

"Sure, he lied about the car being broke down," Ibrahim replied promptly.

"We know that. Anything else?" Rick asked.

The Berber shook his head. "He's not much of a talker, at least on the road."

"You came right from Marrakech to Ouarzazate? You didn't stop anywhere?" Dizzy asked, probing every possibility.

"Only for a few minutes at Taddert, to pick up some cigarettes."

"Who wanted the cigarettes?"

"Hamida. I don't smoke."

"So he got out of the car and went into a souk in Taddert?"

"Yes," Ibrahim said. "On the way back to the car he stopped for a couple of seconds to talk to an old fellow on a donkey. Asked him for a light or something. He wasn't gone more than five minutes in all."

An old fellow on a donkey. Dizzy felt suddenly uneasy, as though once more she were on the brink of discovery. But although Bou Hamida must be a singularly negligent man not to have picked up matches along with his cigarettes there was nothing suspicious in asking a drover for a light.

Or was there? Chevrolets came equipped with automatic lighters, and Hamida should have been trying to reach Ouarzazate before dark if he wanted to sleep anywhere but in the car overnight. "An old fellow on a donkey," Dizzy repeated aloud. "What did he look like? Can you remember, Ibrahim?" To Berbers perhaps all donkey drivers did not look identical, as they did to Americans.

Ibrahim pondered. "He had a gray beard and he was skinny and dark skinned. I think he wore a turban, not a fez, and he was dressed in rags. But there was one curious thing. He had on a pair of new green *babouches*. Not yellow, green. You don't see that color much around Marrakech."

Dizzy clapped her hands together spontaneously, just once, then said, trying to keep her voice from trembling with excitement, "That may be a help, Ibrahim." Delving into her purse, she handed the Berber two five dirham notes. "Here, this should get you back to the city." Then, quickly, she drew Rick and Louella toward the car. "Let's do our best to get loose from here!"

Fourteen

"I'm positive it was the same man," Dizzy told Rick breathlessly. She had relinquished the wheel of the car and was sitting tensely on the front seat beside him, her hands clasped in her lap, her toes clenched inside her shoes. "I saw him three times, but I couldn't have told you why he was different until Ibrahim mentioned the green *babouches*. Then I was sure!"

Rick looked skeptical. "It doesn't mean much, that I can see."

"Within two days I see the same donkey driver at the Bab Agnou Gate, outside the souk where Felicia disappeared, and at the top of Tizi N'Tichka and it doesn't mean much? Do you think that old man's donkey has wings?"

"Look, maybe up around Telouet *all* the Arabs wear green *babouches*."

Telouet! Dizzy raised a hand to her mouth. That's where she had seen him last, on the track leading toward Telouet. Like a lightning flash came the remark that had been eluding her, a remark Bou Hamida had begun to make in the courtyard at Tifoultout. "Isn't this the most beautiful casbah you have ever seen?" she had asked in rapturous innocence, and he had replied, "If you think this is beautiful you should see—" then had broken off short.

"Rick," Dizzy cried, "which is the most beautiful casbah? The most beautiful of all?"

Rick was trying to pass a native bus stopped in the center of the road, where it was unloading still more celebrants for the *moussem*. "How should I know? Telouet's supposed to have been planned on a grand scale and to be as beautiful as a palace inside, but you're jumping from one subject to another like a rubber ball. What gives?"

"Telouet," Dizzy was whispering. "Of course." At last she had unearthed from the recesses of her memory the missing clue. "Telouet! The obvious place."

"Will you please calm down and talk sensibly," Rick begged her as he got clear of the village on the winding road that led into the High Atlas. From the rear Louella added, "You'd best relax, Miss Deborah. This hot sun can be mighty bad for a person's head."

Dizzy laughed and twisted around to pat Louella's plump knee, decently hidden beneath her skirt. "I haven't got sunstroke, honestly. I'm just terribly excited, because I have a very strong hunch Felicia is being held captive at Telouet!"

"You must be kidding," Rick snorted.

"She said 'hunch,' " Louella reminded him, "and you know last time she had a hunch you lost a dollar."

"That's right," Rick admitted. "But please try to be logical, Dizzy. Stop skipping around and tell us in an orderly fashion how you've arrived at this remarkable conclusion."

For once Dizzy didn't mind being patronized, because she sensed beneath Rick's assumed disdain a flicker of hope. "Let me go back to the beginning," she suggested, and proceeded to review her encounters with the green-shod Arab and her recollection of the conversation with Bou Hamida. "Telouet has been abandoned. It's apparently absolutely enormous, and it's off the main road, in a pretty isolated spot. If I were a kidnapper I couldn't think of a better hiding place."

"You sound like the idiot and the stolen horse," Rick groused, but Dizzy knew his interest had been aroused. As the little car climbed higher and higher into the mountains Louella came forth with a proposal. "Patrick, you said next time Miss Deborah had a hunch you'd let her play it. How long would it take to turn off to Telouet?"

"Half an hour there, half an hour back."

"Let's do it. We could still get to Marrakech before sundown," Louella said after checking the time. She began to pass out the sandwiches everyone had forgotten. "Better keep our strength up, because who knows what we may find?"

Who indeed? If I'm taking them up another dead-end street I'll never live it down, Dizzy thought as Rick swung the car from the road into the narrow track where they had stopped two days before for lunch. The scenery at once became wilder, the hills bare and glaring, the roadside vegetation so scarce that no goats or sheep could be seen. In fact, not a living creature was visible—no man or mule, no bird or animal. "I've been higher up in our mountains at home," Dizzy said with a shiver, "but this seems like the top of the world."

"It most surely does," seconded Louella. She sounded overawed by the stark crags that were painted by the sun in strange shades of red, violet, and pinky yellow, while in the distance peaks of cold green or cobalt rose tier on tier.

Then a bend in the track brought the car out to a high plain, and in the distance all three saw a cluster of ghostly spires reaching into the sky, while vultures wheeled and turned upon the air currents above them. Nobody spoke, but everyone knew it was the Casbah of Telouet.

Dizzy shaded her eyes with her hands. "It's enormous!" she breathed, and her heart dropped at the prospect of 600 rooms, in any one of which unimaginable danger might lurk.

The great casbah crouched like a lion high on a barren promontory, while at its feet a sprinkling of shrubs made a spotty carpet of green. As they drew closer, Dizzy could see that each tower was topped by a huge stork's nest and that above the crenellated lookout posts ravens and kites had joined the vultures wheeling against the hard blue sky. Like a witch's castle in a fairy tale the place seemed to emanate evil. Rick frowned and drove on without slowing down. "Well, there you have it," he said.

Dizzy felt her responsibility more keenly with every passing moment. Now that she had dragged them here she was aghast at her own temerity. Even if Felicia should be hidden behind these walls, what could they hope to accomplish—one young girl, one plump cook, and one stout-hearted but inexperienced young man?

Rick pulled up before double doors of iron-bossed wood twenty feet high. The Fiat looked like a child's toy in comparison. "This is your show, Diz. Do we knock or just walk in?"

"We honk," Dizzy decided, but then changed her mind. "No, I'll knock. It will be quieter."

"I'll knock," Rick decided. "You get behind the wheel and if the doors open you drive right through, understand?"

Dizzy nodded meekly, and slid over to the seat Rick vacated. At the sound of the car door shutting a kestrel hawk, disturbed from its nest in the casbah wall, flew out screeching. The sharp, staccato, scolding cries made Dizzy's blood run cold, and Louella muttered, "Hark at that bad-luck bird!"

Rick was hammering on the huge doors, and Dizzy instinctively said, "Sh!" Just then came the reluctant creaking and rasping of rusty hinges, and through a crack an Arab face peered out with expectation which quickly changed to suspicion. "*Fermé*," the old man muttered, and shook his head.

But Rick's shoulder was against the wood. He gave a strong shove and Dizzy caught a glimpse of green *babouches* before both the boy and the man disappeared.

Seconds dragged to a minute. The hawk settled on its nest again and Dizzy's heart hammered. Then, slowly, the great doors opened, and Rick gestured to Dizzy to come ahead. She drove through the entryway without gunning the motor, and parked in the shelter of a high inner wall. The old Arab was rubbing his wrist and repeating, "*Fermé. Fermé aujourd'hui.*"

"Keep an eye on him while I close the gate," Rick commanded as Dizzy got out of the car. Already he was pushing the heavy doors into place and tugging at the bar that held them shut. Dizzy hurried to a spot between the old Arab and the stalls of an open stable on the opposite side of the courtyard. She had spotted a low door beside it that might presumably lead to a caretaker's hut. Although the old fellow seemed feeble she was taking no chances. He might be more spry than he appeared.

The bar dropped into place with a heavy thud as Louella eased herself out of the back seat of the Fiat. "He don't look as if he could harm a fly," she observed.

"Let's play it cool," Rick suggested, "and pretend we're just very determined tourists. Then we can take the old boy with us while we're exploring, and if we run into any of his confederates we'll stand a better chance of—"

Dizzy broke in. "We'll make better time alone. I think we should tie him up and leave him with Louella, somewhere inside. She can keep him quiet, if necessary."

Louella looked as though she didn't relish this role, but she made no objection, because it was quite obvious that she would slow up the exploration party. "What do we have to tie him with?" was all she said.

Rick was wearing beltless slacks and Dizzy was dressed in a shift. They looked at one another in consternation until Dizzy said, "His turban!"

"Of course." Urging the Arab ahead, Rick forced him to unlock the painted wood door to the casbah proper. In a minute all four were in a long, marble-floored hall with anterooms opening on either side, and rubble from a ruined ceiling lying crumbled on the tiles.

Dizzy chose the strongest-looking door and pushed it inward on a dim storeroom lighted sparsely from a slit window set high in the far wall. She beckoned to Rick, who pushed the captive across the threshold, then muttered "Excuse me" as he pulled the turban off the Arab's head.

The old man groaned, but he didn't resist because,

obviously, he was terrified. Rick, with Dizzy's help, made short work of tying him up securely, after tearing off a length of the turban for a possible gag. "If he so much as bleats, shove this in his mouth," Rick told Louella. "And don't open the door on any account until we get back."

Louella looked almost as frightened as the Arab. "You hurry, hear? This place could have rats."

Rick patted her arm and said inaccurately but comfortingly, "Rats don't come out except at night." Then, with Dizzy in the lead, the pair hurried out of the room.

The long hall led to a flight of steps, the steps to another, higher courtyard, with a dry fountain in the center and vestiges of grandeur on every side. Tall, intricately decorated doors led from a surrounding arcade to palatial apartments with ceilings of paneled cedar. Marble pillars with capitals of lacelike plaster rose to support beams that could scarcely hold the heavy ceiling aloft. Most of the magnificent doors stood ajar, sagging on their hinges or ripped free of them by vandals. Gaping holes testified to heavy brass locks torn away and handles wrenched from their places. It took only a cursory inspection to realize that there would be no safe hiding place here.

"Six hundred rooms," Dizzy breathed. "Do you suppose there really are that many?" She had spotted a curving staircase to still another level and was heading toward it with Rick at her heels.

"I hope not," Rick replied in an undertone. "Though they say a thousand men worked on this place."

On the next floor opulence was contrasted by rooms walled with rain-stained white plaster. Here no decoration had been undertaken before the casbah was abandoned to the elements. From a barred window Dizzy could look down into another courtyard, and across to other apartments rising on the far side. Had it not been for a dog barking and a cock crowing persistently in the distance she would have felt that this great castle was a mirage.

Down another flight of steps, slipping over rubble and broken treads, no longer making an effort to keep quiet, Dizzy and Rick skidded. The place seemed completely empty. It was impossible not to fear that they had tied up an innocent caretaker and that the only captive here was the ghost of a Glaoui. Across a second, then a third quadrangle the pair ran, glancing into every cubbyhole, trying each closed door, of which there were many.

Upstairs and down. Downstairs and up. Almond trees, unpruned and spindly, reached above the walls of an abandoned pleasure garden where marble benches crawled with bougainvillea and lily ponds stood empty. Above the trees another huge section of casbah rose, tier upon ruined tier, into the pitiless sky.

"Let's split up," Dizzy proposed. "You take one side. I'll take the other."

"Not on your life," Rick retorted. "I'm not leaving you for one minute by yourself."

"Oh, Rick, you're worse than Louella!" Dizzy complained, as she picked her way up an enclosed stairway to a second-floor balcony. Off this, unexpectedly, were a group of rooms almost intact, the colors of the decoration still bright, the tiled floors as beautiful as ever. "This room could have housed a harem of fifty," Rick said with a whistle. "And the smaller one must have been planned for the favorite."

This last room looked down on a small enclosed *djenan*, planted with trees and flowering bushes that had somehow managed to survive the long years of neglect. Dizzy stood looking about the little garden for several seconds, then hurried back down the stairs and found her way into the enclosure by a side door. Something had attracted her attention, something that was out of place among the overgrown flower beds and the leaf-strewn walks. Debris was to be expected, but—

She bent down and picked up a paper airplane folded from a book page. The paper was cheap, new, and unmarred by mountain rains or winter snows. Even before she opened it up and spread it out she was electrified. It was undeniably a page torn from an American paperback and bore as a running head the wildly improbable title of a mystery by Erle Stanley Gardner—*The Case of the Mythical Monkeys.*

Fifteen

Tingling with excitement, Dizzy wanted to shout "Rick!" but instead she stood galvanized to the spot where she had found the paper. Instinctively her glance moved upward, like a bird who has discovered seeds on the ground and seeks their source.

Up and up, to the top of one of the battlemented towers and a small barred window, from which another scrap of paper was drifting, to be caught on an air current and wafted across the wall. "What are you looking at?" whispered Rick at Dizzy's shoulder, making her start and stagger backward. "Felicia," she whispered in a voice shaking with emotion. "She must be up there!"

With a finger to her lips she held out the wrinkled paper, then pulled Rick into the shadow of the garden wall. For why hadn't Felicia shouted? Why, if she could see them down here in the abandoned garden, didn't she scream out their names in sheer delight?

"There must be a guard."

"Or else they've got her gagged," said Rick, who had digested the evidence of the torn paperback page and was thinking ahead. "How do we get up there, anyway?"

"Softly," returned Dizzy.

"I mean where are the stairs?"

"In the tower, I suppose. One of those spiral staircases. Rick, I wish we had a gun or something. I'm scared."

"Well, I'm glad you are," replied Rick, regarding Dizzy with unexpected affection. "I was beginning to think you were superhuman or something. Come on, we can be scared together, but let's get going!"

Locating the tower stairs from the inside of the casbah took several minutes, but once found they led upward, as Dizzy had predicted, in a spiral. Recently swept clean of fallen plaster, the treads were in fair condition, so it was possible to mount quietly, but less than halfway up both Dizzy and Rick had to stop to catch their breath. It was a long way to the top.

They realized that if they were surprised by an attacker from above he would have the advantage. The space was too narrow for two people to walk abreast. Elbow room, even for one, was scant.

For some time now they had been ascending in the dark, because the light from the lower door had long since petered out. Dizzy felt her way along behind Rick, and wished futilely for a flashlight. She made every effort to keep absolutely quiet, but even her breathing seemed loud. From time to time her hand, feeling along the tower wall, encountered a cobweb, and she recoiled, hating spiders as much as Louella hated rats.

At last a ray of light from above penetrated the stairwell, flickering on Rick's strained, apprehensive face and touching Dizzy's hair with gold. More cautiously than ever the pair crept onward, step after slow careful step. Then suddenly and uncontrollably Rick sneezed.

Dizzy moved flat against the wall, her distaste for cobwebs forgotten, and Rick made the last few steps at a bound. At the sound of a grunt, then a scuffle, Dizzy plucked up her courage and raced for the top in time to see Rick deliver a well-aimed blow to a bearded chin.

The Arab staggered backward against the wall, scowling but not badly hurt. Dizzy could see at a glance that he was a strong young fellow, probably a peasant from these mountains. Recovering, he lurched forward angrily and caught Rick just under the left eye. Then the pair began circling like animals in the cramped space.

This, Dizzy realized, put Rick at a disadvantage. Accustomed to fist-fighting in the American manner, he needed elbow room. On the other hand, the Arab was hampered by his long jellaba. Caught off guard, he had no chance to rid himself of the cumbersome garment, and now it wrapped itself around his legs.

Rick feinted, and reached the Arab's nose with a neat left. He had his back to Dizzy and she was subconsciously aware that his shoulders were broad for his height and that the muscles in his arms were big. The Arab, blood spurting from his injured nose, set his feet and brought a haymaker to the point of Rick's chin. Dizzy could hear the crack of his head against the wall, and for a second it seemed that he might go down, but he recovered and closed in like a wrestler, grabbing for the Arab's right wrist.

Then Dizzy saw the knife. It glinted in the light, a silver-handled dagger that looked sharp. At once she screamed, screamed at the top of her lungs, and for a split second the Arab glanced toward the stairwell. It was time enough.

With a quick twist of the man's wrist, Rick sent the knife spinning, and Dizzy reached for it as it skidded toward her. At the same moment Rick began to swing rights and lefts in a windmill that proved baffling to his opponent. Although there was no doubt that the guard was the stronger of the two he seemed to feel helpless, once disarmed, and when Rick shoved him back against an arched wooden door and hit him a tremendous right punch he collapsed in a groggy heap.

Like an avenging angel Dizzy was upon him, her hair haloed by the sun, the knife held high over her head. "Don't you dare move!" she cried.

"Hey, give me that thing!" Rick gasped. "You might hurt somebody." He seized the knife from her hand

and stood looking down at it, appalled, while from the other side of the heavy wooden door came Felicia's voice, only a trifle less calm than usual.

"What's going on out there?"

"I'm trying to keep Dizzy from killing the guard," Rick responded, relief making him prattle nonsense. He pulled the Arab away from the door while Dizzy tried the handle. It was locked, of course.

"Felicia, does he have a key?" Dizzy called, her mouth to the keyhole.

"No. The woman keeps it."

"What woman?"

"The caretaker's wife."

The Arab was beginning to stir, so Rick made a straightjacket out of his jellaba, pulling it down from his shoulders and ripping the back to the waist so that he could tie it around the man's pinioned arms.

"How many more are there?" Dizzy asked Felicia.

"Just the old couple and the guard, I think."

Belatedly Dizzy inquired, "Are you all right?"

"Oh, yes," Felicia replied. "I'm fine."

"Well, hang on a few more minutes and we'll get you out of here," Rick promised.

Then Dizzy spoke again. "Do you know where the woman keeps the key?"

"In her apron pocket, probably."

Dizzy groaned. By the time they could find the caretaker's quarters, overpower the woman, and find the key the Arab would surely have recovered sufficiently to wriggle free of his rather flimsy bonds. Since the guard was wearing a crotcheted cap rather than a turban, they had no truly adequate way of tying him up. Then an alternate idea occurred to her. She poked at the door with a fingernail, then said, "Rick, this wood is thick but it's old and spongy. Try cutting around the keyhole with that knife."

"Bright girl! Stand back, Sis."

"I'm nowhere near the door," Felicia replied calmly.

Rick jabbed with the knife point, pulled it from the wood with little effort, and jabbed again. "You're a genius," he praised Dizzy as he managed to make a small opening, then carved away at the sides of the hole.

The entire job took less than ten minutes. When the aperture was large enough to admit Dizzy's hand, she reached through and turned the brass handle from the inside. A second later Rick followed her through the door into a semi-circular tower room bare of furnishings except for an old-fashioned commode, a wash basin and pitcher, and a black goatskin rug piled with gaudy velvet pillows. Felicia was lying on the rug propped on one arm, an open book at her elbow.

"Hi, Diz," she said. "Rick, you're getting a black eye!"

"You should see the other fellow," Rick retorted with a rueful grin. "What are you doing lounging around like Scheherazade while we risk life and limb to rescue you?"

"They've put me in irons," explained Felicia, lifting an ankle to which was fastened a thick metal bracelet, attached to a chain that ended in a ring set into the tiled floor. "Do you think you can pry me loose?"

Dizzy was horrified, but Rick, oddly enough, seemed fascinated. "I thought they only had these things in dungeons."

"Well," said Felicia, "this is an attic dungeon."

Already Rick had knelt and was pounding at the tiles with the handle of the Arab's knife. The ceramic chipped quite readily, but beneath was a solid block of concrete into which the ring was set.

"There's a key to this thing somewhere," Felicia said plausibly. "Maybe the guard has it. You could look."

While Rick was searching his erstwhile opponent, Dizzy banged ineffectually away at the floor. To be balked at this eleventh hour seemed unjust. She examined the chain, which was rusty but strong, while Felicia observed, "There's no use trying to pick the lock. I've tried that, and it's hopeless."

Rick came back in the room, shaking his head. "Nope, he hasn't got it."

"It can't be a big key," said Dizzy impatiently. "Maybe they leave it nearby on a hook or something."

Together she and Rick searched the room, but the walls were bare and the window shutters were empty of any extraneous objects. Dizzy felt along the top of the curving door lintel but only got her fingers soiled. "Try *outside* the door," Felicia suggested.

Dizzy went into the passage reluctantly, because the bound guard was a bloody and unpleasant sight. She couldn't help glancing his way, however, and she realized his eyes were fastened, not on her, but on a spot above the door. At once they slid away and regarded her malevolently, but the glance she had apprehended made her search thoroughly. "I've got it!" she cried as her fingers touched a small piece of metal. Triumphantly she carried the key into the room.

It was the work of a few seconds to fit it into the lock and free Felicia, who got to her feet stiffly, then leaned down to gather up her straw basket and the half-finished book.

"Forget that stuff, Sis," Rick scolded. "We've got to beat it before our luck runs out."

With a parting glance at the struggling guard Rick plummeted down the stairs with the girls close behind. He held the Arab's knife gingerly in one hand. Instead of the weapon giving him confidence its possession seemed to alarm him. "Why don't you throw that thing away?" Felicia asked.

"Because I want it for a keepsake," Rick retorted. "It's a trophy of the only fight I've ever won."

Dizzy said, "Sh. Keep quiet, you two. We're not out of here yet." Nor was the way out easy to find. The great casbah was a maze of apartments and gardens, courtyards and palatial rooms. Keeping the position of the sun firmly in mind, Rick led his followers as directly as possible toward the entranceway, but often they came to a dead end and had to retrace their steps.

Like those of most volatile people, Dizzy's moods were fleeting, and elation at Felicia's release quickly gave way to fresh anxiety. Suppose her roommate's guess had been wrong? Suppose the old caretaker and his wife were not the only accomplices of the kidnappers stationed here?

Her misgiving grew as they approached a corner that turned into the final corridor of anterooms where Louella kept guard over the caretaker. Once more Dizzy raised a finger to her lips as her ears detected the sound of footsteps crunching on the gravelly floor. Her heart leaped to her throat and she put out a detaining arm. "Wait!" she cautioned, moving her lips without making a sound.

Rick and Felicia froze as the footsteps became louder. Slow, deliberate, they approached the corner inexorably. There was no time to run, and no place to run to, except back into the unhealthy labyrinth of the casbah. Rick looked down at the knife he held in his hand and his jaw tensed. Then an earsplitting female scream rent the air, a crash and clatter accompanying it. All three peered around the angle of the wall, their terror forgotten, to see Louella holding an Arab woman in a determined bear hug while a trayful of dishes and their steaming contents mingled with the debris on the floor.

Felicia burst out laughing. "That's the caretaker's wife, Louella. She won't hurt you. She's twice as scared as you are. Just look!"

The woman was indeed trembling pathetically, and when Louella's plump arms released her she almost slipped to the floor. "Felicia!" the cook cried. "My land, are you a sight for sore eyes! You all right, child? You ain't hurt?"

"Save your questions for the ride home," Rick ordered peremptorily. He grasped the Arab woman's arm and hustled her into the anteroom where her husband was secured by his own turban. The sight of him elicited another scream, followed by a low, keening sound. "It'll take her five minutes to untie those knots," Rick predicted, "and by then we'll be on our way."

The Fiat stood safely where it had been parked. Louella drew Felicia into the back seat as Rick ran to open the high exit doors. To save time, Dizzy turned the car around and headed toward them, then stopped and slid over to let Rick get behind the wheel.

So far, so good.

The track snaked down the mountainside from Telouet, narrow but clear. For a couple of miles ahead its serpentine length was visible; then it disappeared behind a ridge. Rick drove skillfully and as fast as he dared, while Louella closed her eyes and clutched Felicia's arm. As the lesser of two evils, she was apparently determined to bear with the speed.

Until they were truly out of danger, nobody seemed inclined to talk. Once they reached the highway and were past the village of Taddert, Dizzy felt sure they would all take heart, but along this circuitous route through the bald mountains she sat tense and silent, wishing they could go home by helicopter rather than by car.

"Relax, Dizzy," Rick advised. "We're going to be O.K. now."

But she couldn't relax. It was useless to try. She was still dogged by uneasiness, as though around the next bend some unforeseen disaster might lurk.

"Ooops!" Rick hugged the inside of the road, scraping a fender on the cliff as a car swerved around a steep curve in second gear. It clung to the outside track, laboring past them on the upward climb, a green Chevrolet that was instantly recognizable.

Bou Hamida and Rick saw each other at the same instant, but neither dared risk an accident. Felicia was so busy trying to pacify Louella that she scarcely noticed the passing car, but Dizzy breathed in alarm, "He saw us!"

Rick nodded grimly, but he didn't speak, and it was apparent that he didn't want to inform his sister and Louella of this new complication. Instead he concentrated on the road like the driver of a racing car. The little Fiat swayed from side to side as it plunged through the tortuous hills.

Dizzy also sat silent, trying to remember where a widening of the track might allow Hamida to swing the bulky Chevy around. He wouldn't dare try to turn on a curve, or would he? There was not the slightest doubt in either her mind or Rick's—of this she was sure!—that their false friend would make every effort to overtake them. And with superior engine power and a lighter load there was little doubt he would succeed.

Dizzy began to count the kilometer marks, attempting to calm her raveled nerves. Rick glanced toward her as they careered onto the highway and she reached over and touched his arm to indicate that she was with him—all the way. In the back seat Louella had begun to moan, unaware of new danger but convinced that Rick's reckless driving would kill them all. Felicia continued to try to comfort her, but as the car hurtled through Taddert's one street she said, "Don't you think you'd better slow down a little, Rick?"

Her brother shook his head. "You'd better tell them, Diz."

"We passed Bou Hamida on the track back there. He's bound to overtake us if he tries."

"And he'll try," decided Felicia. She put her arm around Louella's shoulders and said, "There, there. Rick will do the best he can."

"Maybe there's police in this village," the cook gathered herself together to suggest.

"If there are, they'll be after us, and that's a good thing," Rick muttered, but Dizzy felt that this hope was idle. Such a small mountain village could scarcely support officers of the law. Far more likely it would house another of Hamida's confederates.

From Taddert on down to the Haouz plain the road

cut through the Atlas in a series of switchbacks, visible at great distances from one mountain to another, although the turn directly ahead was usually blind. Rick leaned on his horn before taking each curve, but he braked only when he went by a laboring bus bound in the opposite direction up the grade. Speed was their only hope.

Dipping into a green valley, the road climbed the opposite ridge, and now the heavily laden Fiat began to crawl upward in low gear. Dizzy sat with hands clenched, scanning the ribbon of road they had just traveled. Near the top, on the very spine of the mountain, she spotted the green car.

Hamida was perhaps five minutes behind them, and coming down fast, like a skier on a slalom course. From this ridge the Chevrolet looked like a toy, equipped with a speedy motor and started on a miniature racetrack.

"Look!" Dizzy pointed. "Here he comes."

Felicia and Louella peered out of the open window, but Rick merely grunted. He was completely engaged by the Fiat, which was beginning to gasp and choke, even in low. With every passing second the Chevy gained ground as the smaller car chugged slowly along. Each car was equally visible to the other. Only the hazards around the next curve were concealed.

On these Rick was concentrating, but Dizzy's eyes followed Bou Hamida's headlong drive around the hairpin turns with the fascination she might have felt for an advancing cobra. Moving upward toward him in the same laborious manner it had evidenced in going by the Fiat a short time previously was the native bus, piled high with bicycles and bundles and crowded as was usual with people. Like a leviathan it rumbled onward, keeping doggedly to the middle of the narrow road, while Dizzy caught her breath and her heart almost stopped.

"The bus! He can't see it!"

Now even Rick glanced toward the opposite ridge. And in that same instant Bou Hamida rounded a sharp curve, appearing directly in the path of the bus.

Too far away to seem believable, the accident might have taken place on a movie screen. There was a sudden screech of brakes, but the Chevy didn't halt. It caromed off the edge of the cliff and bounced, rolling over twice to land on its side, precariously lodged against an outcrop of rock.

At a fortuitous turnout Rick pulled over and parked, while everyone climbed out, deeply shocked in spite of their relief. "Do you suppose he's been killed?" Felicia asked.

It was a question nobody could answer. The bus had stopped, and its passengers were pouring out like ants. Dizzy could see several men slipping and sliding down the rocky bank toward the wrecked car. They began tugging and pulling at a limp figure, then dislodged a cascade of rocks as they scrambled out of the way.

A moment later the Chevrolet burst into flames.

Sixteen

It was evening in Marrakech, an evening turned blissfully cool after a languid summer day. In the garden of the Harding villa sat Dizzy and Felicia, watching the last flights of egrets hurry to their roosts in the wool souks before the stars came out.

Rick came through the open doors from the library and flung himself into a chair. "That's a good letter from Mother," he said to Felicia. "I'm glad Aunt Janet is so much better, but I don't see any reason for Mum to hurry back. We're making out just fine."

Dizzy smiled to herself. She wondered how Mrs. Harding would react to the events of the week which, from the perspective of another four days, seemed strangely remote. Only Rick's silver-handled knife and the chafed skin on Felicia's right ankle testified to the reality of the kidnapping.

Ali came out to the terrace, bowed and announced dinner, which brought Felicia to her feet more quickly than usual. "I'm hungry," she declared.

"What's the matter, didn't they feed you well in your tower, Rumpelstiltskin?"

"Rick, you're incorrigible. Rumpelstiltskin was the dwarf, not the girl with the golden hair. As a matter of fact the food wasn't too bad, just monotonous. And that poor woman was very kind."

On the dining table candles flickered on either side of a great bowl of roses. From the open windows came the scent of jasmine and the croaking of a frog in the lily pond. Dizzy sighed happily and slipped into the chair Rick held. Fairy tales made appropriate talk for this glamorous setting, with the shining silver and the candlelight playing on Felicia's serene face.

There was melon, then a chicken potpie carried in proudly by Louella. "Your daddy ought to be here," she said as she put it down in front of Rick. "He likes this better than roast beef." Then, at the sound of gravel crunching on the drive, she moved over to the window. "My land, that's positively spooky. Here he comes now!"

A car door slammed and Dr. Harding materialized in the dining-room door like a genie from a bottle. "Well, isn't this a happy little family," he cried. "Where's your mother?"

Rick explained and Dr. Harding nodded quickly. "I've got great news," he said, "but let me get a shower and climb into some clean clothes. I've come all the way from Mhamid today. Save me some of that potpie,

Rick, and congratulations, Louella, on your timing. I'll be right back."

Ali laid another place and Louella rescued the pie from Rick's imminent attack. "I'll just pop it in the oven until the professor gets down," she said. "It won't hurt it a bit."

Fifteen minutes later it was Dr. Harding who served the young people with generous portions. He was tired but ebullient, and he told them immediately that the oil shots were a great success.

"Everything we'd hoped for," he said happily. "Dr. Hazziz and the King will be delighted. Considering the complications we ran into, I'm delighted too."

Dizzy sat politely silent while Dr. Harding talked, but she found it curious that he didn't mention Bou Hamida's defection or Rick's message at the Hotel du Sud in Zagora. The note should have told him of the kidnapping, and she would have thought this his first concern.

Apparently Rick's thoughts were traveling the same route. "Pop, didn't you get my note?"

"What note? Where?"

"In Zagora."

"How did you know I was in Zagora? I was booked to pick up a jeep in Tinerhir."

Rick nodded. "We were there, too."

"*You* were there? But why?"

"Well, you see Felicia was kidnapped and we were

trying to catch up with you, but now I guess it's just as well we didn't, since everything's turned out all right."

Dr. Harding cast penetrating eyes on his daughter. "Has Patrick been out in the sun without a hat?" he asked.

The question made Felicia giggle. "I knew he wouldn't believe it," she said to Rick. "We'd better tell you everything that's happened, Father, right from the day after you left."

Ali came in, cleared the table and brought dessert, but everyone ate abstractedly as Felicia started the story with the account of her abduction in the souk.

"Dizzy was trying on a gold-embroidered caftan—he called it the caftan of a little princess, remember?—and I went to the door to look at another one in the daylight. When I came back she passed out cold, but even then I thought it was the heat and the heavy caftan. With all the whodunits I've read I should have suspected the tea was drugged," Felicia shrugged apologetically.

"You had just seen something peculiar outside," Dizzy reminded her. "You never told me what."

"Didn't I? It was Bou Hamida talking to that donkey driver with the green *babouches* who passed us in the Bab Agnou Gate. I didn't know until the same man turned up on the trip to Telouet, but of course they were plotting together. It was Hamida *being* there I thought odd, especially when he'd sent Rick and the Countess off to Amizmiz."

Dr. Harding passed a hand over his forehead. "Children," he begged, "could you be a little more orderly about all this?"

Felicia began again, and described the small boy who had lured them to the souk and had fetched the mint tea. "You know there's always one boy who's more persistent than the rest, Father. We were just bound to follow him."

"So Dizzy fainted. Then what?" asked Dr. Harding, despairing of a consecutive report.

"Then this man acted scared and said she should lie down, and I helped carry her into a back room where I thought we would find a couch, but there was only a pile of rugs. I guess I hadn't drunk my tea as fast as she had. Besides I'm bigger, and the drug took longer."

"But it did work?"

"Oh, yes. Otherwise I'd remember something more. The next thing I knew I was wrapped in an old jellaba so my hair wouldn't show, being driven along somewhere in the mountains. It was after dark when we got to Telouet."

She went on to describe her imprisonment in the tower, the ministrations of the frightened but kindly woman, and the guard posted at the door. Then Rick took over the story and told his father about the frantic effort to overtake him and bring him home.

"Which is just what Hamida wanted, of course," Dr. Harding said.

"We know that now, but how did you learn he was working against you?" Rick asked.

"Well, Mokhtar wasn't a very savory character," Dr. Harding said with a wry grin, "and I was mad as hops about the delay. I made an educated guess that there never was a jeep available, and that Hamida had led me up a dead-end street. That was when I decided to ditch him, even if he should show up."

"So you told him off by not revealing where you were headed next," Felicia murmured. "Dizzy and Rick told me all about that."

One after another the details were related; the encounter with Bou Hamida at Tifoultout, Louella's conversation with the bus driver from Zagora, Dizzy's inspired deduction that Mr. Wheel was Mr. Huile, the *imam's* assurance that Dr. Harding had found extra help and another jeep to take into the desert, the clues which led the young people to Telouet.

"It was Dizzy, again, who found the paper airplane," Rick said admiringly. "But for this roommate of yours, Sis, you might still be languishing in chains."

"It wasn't so bad," Felicia said soothingly to her father. "I had a lot to read."

"Speaking of that airplane," Dizzy broke in, "I've been meaning to ask you how you got it through the grating. You weren't anywhere within reach."

"I flew it," said Felicia.

"You what?" asked Rick.

"I made dozens of airplanes and flew them toward the window. A few sailed through the bars and the woman gathered up the rest. She thought I was just slightly addlepated. Clever, don't you think?"

Dizzy burst out laughing. "Felicia, you're the limit!"

Dr. Harding looked as though he agreed. "The old fellow with the green *babouches*. Was he the real caretaker?"

"I don't think so," Felicia replied, "although I can't be sure. I never actually saw him after we reached the casbah, but he was along on the ride up from Marrakech. So was his wife."

"Sounds like a real gang," her father observed.

"Oh, it was," Rick assured him. "There was even one of our own gardeners in on it, Ali says. Somehow they forced him to keep tabs on the movements of everyone in the family. He quit his job a couple of days after we took off."

Dizzy remembered the cry in the night that had so alarmed her and wondered whether this wasn't perhaps connected with the gardener's defection. It seemed reasonable to assume that the Communists might have applied pressure—painful pressure!—to extract the information they needed from a workman who was disinclined to cooperate.

She suggested this, and Dr. Harding agreed with her

reasoning. "I wondered whether you had figured out that the Russians were involved," he said. "You see we quite expected they would try to hold us back—that's why it didn't especially surprise me to discover Hamida was a traitor in our camp; but I never dreamed they'd go so far as to involve my family." He looked at Felicia as though she were extremely precious and said, "I'm terribly, terribly sorry, dear."

"Oh, it wasn't your fault, Father. And don't be too concerned. I had quite an adventure, really. Something to tell my grandchildren about."

"I'm only sorry about one thing," Rick broke in. "I think the Countess should have gone with us to the police. She could have made them understand."

Dr. Harding appeared thoughtful. "She was acting according to her lights," he countered. "Odette is very French in temperament, and she understands the intricacies of Moroccan political intrigue better than the rest of us. To precipitate an international incident would seem to her the height of folly. In her view I was the only one who could deal with such a bizarre situation, so she sent you hotfooting off to bring me back."

"In other words she played straight into Communist hands."

"I'm afraid so, but at the same time she was trying to protect American interests. Don't forget that."

"And you think she's completely loyal?"

"Odette? Utterly, Patrick, utterly." There was no doubt whatever in Dr. Harding's tone, only amusement.

"There's another thing behind her disenchantment with the police," he added. "When the Countess first came to this country, as a young widow, she accepted an invitation to dine rather late one evening in the Fez medina with a handsome Moroccan guide. You know how these dinners drag on, and it was almost midnight when the man—who was quite courteous and proper, by the way—got her back to her hotel. Imagine her surprise when she discovered that her absence had caused a great hue and cry! The police had been alerted and hauled both the guide and the Countess off to jail. It took until dawn to make the point that the guide had meant no harm, but even so the poor fellow lost his license. As a result Odette has a very poor opinion of the constabulary."

Rick was satisfied and went on to describe the actual escape from Telouet, not omitting the amusing incident of Louella, who had disobeyed orders and stalked out into the corridor to take a captive of her own. When he came to the wild ride down from the Tizi N'Tichka, however, he faltered. "Even admitting Hamida was a scoundrel, still it was terrible to see him go over that cliff."

"Of course it was," agreed his father. "Have you found out whether he survived?"

Rick shook his head. "But I do wish we could call the hospital now."

"Why not? Hamida's still in my employ, so far as

anyone else knows. Inquiring about the accident would be the most natural thing in the world."

Rick pushed back his chair. "I'll do it right now."

But his father said, "Wait! Let's do it the American way, through the police." His eyes twinkled. "*I'm* not afraid of provoking an international incident!"

He need not have feared. The law officer who was sent to the villa the next morning had never been farther from Marrakech than Casablanca. Diplomatic relations between Morocco and the United States didn't interest him in the least. He clucked his teeth unhappily over the report of the kidnapping, but once he learned that Miss Harding was safe and sound, back home and blooming, he was ready to wash his hands of the entire matter.

Dr. Harding, however, was persistent. He learned, through a telephone call made by the policeman, that Bou Hamida was on the critical list in the hospital, that he had undergone a severe concussion and had three broken ribs, but that there was considerable likelihood he would pull through.

"When the time comes we'll prosecute," Dizzy heard Dr. Harding say. "Kidnapping is a crime that should never go unpunished, and I intend to see to it that Hamida and his gang are rounded up."

"Yes sir, yes sir," agreed the representative of the constabulary, who looked cowed by such a tough

American attitude. He backed out of the library bowing, and murmuring "*Inch' Allah.*"

Outside, Rick was helping Ali unpack the Land Rover and stow away the equipment. In the kitchen Louella was baking a fresh peach pie. Upstairs Felicia was writing to a boy who was moving on from Andover to Harvard in the fall and whom she hoped to interest in taking her to football games. Dizzy wandered out to the garden with a leftover breakfast roll that she crumbled for the peacock. A new gardener, sweeping the walks with a reed broom, looked at the bird with an expression that said, as clearly as though he had spoken, "Spoiled!" Then he grinned at the little blond houseguest and nodded. It was another lazy summer day, and all was well.

At dinner that same evening Dr. Harding reported on a telephone chat with his wife. She was coming home on the Saturday plane and her sister would follow in a week or so, to recuperate in the leisurely atmosphere of Marrakech.

Dizzy was reminded of one question she had failed to ask. "Felicia, did you take the note with your mother's Paris address from under the flower bowl on the hall table?"

Felicia shook her head. "No. Did it disappear?"

"At about the same time you did," Dizzy replied. "Hamida's spy, I suppose."

"That's one thing we'll never know," Rick teased.

"Unless our supersleuth has a clue she isn't talking about."

"No clues. Not even much interest," Dizzy admitted. It was impossible, in real life, to wrap everything up in a neat little package. The mystery had been solved. She was looking ahead, not back.

"What are you all doing tonight?" Dr. Harding interrupted her reverie by asking.

Rick answered promptly. "I'm taking Diz dancing on the roof of that new hotel."

Involuntarily both Dizzy and Dr. Harding glanced at Felicia, who regarded them in amusement. "Don't worry about me," she said cheerfully. "I've got a good book."

It was Christmas in Connecticut, and Dizzy had almost finished opening her presents. The living room was awash with gay wrapping paper and discarded ribbons, which her mother, whose sense of duty was considerable, had resisted gathering up.

Before a crackling open fire of pine logs Mr. Driscoll was contentedly trying on a new ski parka, while Nancy exclaimed happily over a pair of skates. Having saved her most exciting present until last, because it had a foreign postmark, Dizzy picked up a fat package wrapped in brown paper and unearthed a pair of scissors with which to cut the cord.

Still she hesitated. Marrakech, Morocco. The address

seemed insubstantial, yet the nine-hundred-year-old city appeared in her mind's eye, clear and sharp. Medieval ramparts and ten great gates. Mosques with green-tiled domes and the wail of the muezzins at first light. Purple bougainvillea spilling over red walls. The insistent cry of "*Balek, balek.*" Arab women in gray jellabas and black-lace nose veils. A fez, a turban, a bearded face. The chorus line in the Casbah of Tifoultout. Felicia in her attic dungeon. Rick. . . .

Rick was coming tomorrow to spend part of his Christmas vacation with the Driscolls. The thought brought Dizzy back to the present and made her heart leap in anticipation.

"Hurry up, Diz! Open it!" her sister begged.

Quickly Dizzy cut the cord.

Inside was a card, signed by all of the Hardings, and out of the inner wrappings spilled a waterfall of gold.

" 'The caftan of a little princess,' " read Dizzy aloud, " 'with all our love to a supersleuth.' "

Eyes filling with tears of surprise and delight, she spread out the evening wrap she would always treasure. "It's the same one–the very same one!" she said. "I wonder how they ever managed to buy it?"

"That's one mystery Rick can probably solve," said her mother.

"Yes," murmured Dizzy. "*Inch' Allah.*" Getting to her feet she held the shining caftan in front of her. "Isn't it perfectly beautiful? Isn't *everything* perfectly beautiful!" she cried.